MICHAEL COLLINS

EITHNE MASSEY has written eight books for children, most of them inspired by Irish history and myth. Many of her books contain elements of fantasy, but like *Tomi*, her most recent book, *Michael Collins: Hero and Rebel* is firmly rooted in historical fact. She is also the author of *Legendary Ireland*, a collection of stories and essays for adults, based on Irish legends and the places connected with them. She is currently working on a book which explores the legends and lore of the Irish seasons.

OTHER CHILDREN'S BOOKS BY EITHNE MASSEY
Best-Loved Irish Legends   *The Dreaming Tree*
Irish Legends: Newgrange, Tara and the Boyne Valley   *The Silver Stag of Bunratty*
Blood Brother, Swan Sister   *Where the Stories Sing*
The Secret of Kells   *Tomi*

MICHAEL
Hero and Rebel
COLLINS

EITHNE MASSEY

THE O'BRIEN PRESS
DUBLIN

First published 2020 by The O'Brien Press Ltd,
12 Terenure Road East, Rathgar, Dublin 6, D06 HD27, Ireland.
Tel: +353 1 4923333; Fax: +353 1 4922777
E-mail: books@obrien.ie
Website: www.obrien.ie
The O'Brien Press is a member of Publishing Ireland.

ISBN: 978-1-78849-210-2

7 6 5 4 3 2 1
24 23 22 21 20

Printed in the UK by Clays Ltd, Elcograf S.p.A.

The paper in this book is produced using pulp from managed forests.

Published in:

Timeline of Main Events

1890 – Michael Collins is born in Woodfield, near Clonakilty in Co. Cork

1906 – Michael moves to London to take up a job in the Kensington Post Office.

1916 – Michael takes part in the 1916 Rising as one of the Volunteers. He is arrested and sent to Britain, where he spends some months in the Frongoch Internment Camp in Wales. He is released at Christmas.

1917 – In February, Michael takes up the post as Secretary of the National Aid Association and Volunteer Dependents' Fund. He also begins to campaign for Sinn Féin candidates in by-elections and to set up his intelligence network. He meets Kitty Kiernan.

1918 – Michael is active in the Volunteer Dependents' Fund, Sinn Féin and the IRB. With Harry Boland, he organises the escape of Éamon de Valera from Lincoln Jail. In November, World War I ends. In the elections that follow, Sinn Féin gain a majority of seats. Michael is elected an MP for Cork.

1919 – In January, the First Dáil is held. Michael becomes Minister of Finance. The War of Independence begins.

1920 – Guerrilla war in Ireland intensifies, with raids, shootings, arrests and hunger strikes. The Auxiliaries and the Black and Tans are sent to Ireland to support the local government forces. Michael sets up 'The Squad'. On 21 November, Bloody Sunday sees a death toll of thirty-two.

1921 – Truce takes effect on 11 July. Michael is sent to London as one of the delegates for the Anglo-Irish Treaty negotiations. The Treaty is signed by the delegates on 6 December.

1922 – In January, the Treaty is ratified by the Dáil. De Valera and the Anti-Treaty members walk out of the Dáil in protest. Michael becomes Leader of the Provisional Government and Arthur Griffith President of the Dáil.

Also in January, the British Army leaves Ireland, and Dublin Castle is handed over to the Free State, represented by Michael.

In June, the Civil War begins. The Four Courts is shelled. Michael becomes Commander-in-Chief of the Free State Army.

In August, Michael is killed in an ambush at Béal na Blá (the Mouth of/Way to the Pasture) in Cork.

Table of Contents

At the Forge, 1900

His head was spinning. Sprawled on the ground, he could already feel the bump rising on his skull. Beneath him he could feel wet, sticky mud. His chest hurt. On top of him was the weight of the world and he was breathing in the sour smell of a boy who hadn't changed his clothes since their first day back at school.

'Surrender! Surrender!'

'Never!'

He pushed with all his might and the weight shifted, lifted, fell to one side. As he struggled to get up, gasping for breath, he heard a sudden roar. Now there was another pain. His ear was caught in a tight grip and he was pulled to his feet.

'Ye young divils!'

The Master, Denis Leary, was pulling him away from Gerry. 'Enough of that now, the pair of you ... Gerry Cadogan – you big amadán, you should know better than to be fighting with the little fellas. And as for you, Michael Collins, are you mad, taking him on? Get inside, the pair of you, and count yourselves lucky not to get a beating to add to your bruises.'

Michael's mouth opened, ready to explain that Gerry Cadogan had been picking on Paddy, the smallest child in the school. The Master was having none of it.

'Amn't I after telling you to get inside, Michael Collins? And not another word out of you or you will be more than sorry!'

Michael went inside.

He settled at his desk, still red with fury that the fight had been interrupted. His sister Katie sent him a sympathetic wink from the girls' side of the classroom. Katie wouldn't tell on him at home. Katie never did.

He nursed his head and felt a sense of injustice grow inside him. Tears were rising, not because of the pain but because of the unfairness of it all. He knew he had been right to take on Gerry Cadogan, the biggest bully in the school. The master should have realised that. Gerry was always picking on the little ones, the ones smaller than Michael, who, although he was only ten, was big and strong. And always ready for a scrap.

There was no arguing with the Master, though Michael had often tried. In spite of this, Michael liked Master O'Leary, and he knew that he was one of his favourite pupils. Master O'Leary took the time every day to tell the stories that Michael loved. Nothing was said, but the children somehow knew that these stories were not to be mentioned when the Inspector came around. They were tales of the heroes of Ireland's past, men like Wolfe Tone and Robert Emmet who had fought against the English. So many battles for Irish freedom from the British Empire! So many failures and executions and betrayals! But every execution and betrayal was the source of another story, another song. The Master taught them the songs and the poems too: poems about brave rebel leaders and noble ancient chieftains. The lines stayed in Michael's head, replayed again and again like music: the calls to battle, the curses piled on the enemy. *May the hearthstone of hell be his best bed forever!* He muttered the curse under his breath and glared at Gerry, pleased to see that there was a fine purple bruise rising on his enemy's face.

The Master wasn't the only one who talked to Michael about standing up to English landlords. Two of his uncles had been sent to jail because they had taken on a landlord who had destroyed their crops, riding through their fields during a hunt. It wasn't right that landlords could do what they liked. It wasn't right that they could take food out of the country, while the people who grew the food were left hungry. The food was sold for the profit of the people who owned the land, not for the benefit of those who worked that land night and day, every day of the year. It wasn't fair and it had to be stopped. Michael sighed. Wasn't that what he had tried to do when he took on Gerry Cadogan?

The Master came down and gave him a friendly cuff on the shoulder. He held an armful of test papers, and slapped one

11

down on Michael's desk. 'There, top of the class in arithmetic again! Well done. Now take that puss off your face. I know what you want to say, but you can't take on the world. Not yet anyway!'

The bell rang for home time and the children streamed out of the school. Rain was lashing down in sheets as Katie and Michael huddled at the gate of the schoolyard. They would be soaked during the two-mile walk back to Woodfield.

Katie knew better than to mention the bruises on Michael's arms or the scratches on his face. One of their Woodfield neighbours joined them.

'Are the two of you off home?' he asked.

Michael shook his head. 'I'm in no rush to get there. And the rain is a good excuse to stop by the forge until it stops!'

Eugene grinned.

'So you reckon your mother has found out about your granny's cloak?

Michael looked sheepish. It had seemed such a good idea at the time, using the heavy woollen cloak as a tent in one of their games. But unfortunately it had ended up getting caught in a fence on their way back to the house. There was now a huge rip in the lining and the hood had lost half its ruffles. The cow dung it had dropped into when they tried to pull it free hadn't helped either.

Katie threw her eyes up to heaven.

'It's going to be worse than you thought, Michael; one of the O'Heas saw the fight you were in with Gerry, so that news will get home to Mam before you do! And she won't be happy when she sees the mud all over your coat.'

Michael scowled. That was the problem with Woodfield. You could do nothing without everybody knowing about it.

Once inside the forge, Michael forgot about the scolding that would no doubt be waiting for him when he got home. The forge was one of his favourite places. It was always full of noise and life, a place where people could come and talk at ease about how the country's affairs were going, and what might be needed to set things right. The old battles were remembered and the politics of the day were discussed. It was always warm in the forge, because the blacksmith, Jimmy, needed to keep a huge fire going for his work. Jimmy himself was red-faced and strong as an ox. Though he never stopped working, he was always happy to have people drop in – even small boys like Michael, who were simply told to keep their mouths shut and their ears open if they wanted to be allowed to stay.

Jimmy's father had forged pikes for rebellions against English rule and his grandfather had fought in 1798. These were the heroes of the old songs and the stories. And now there were other heroes to talk about. One of these was Michael Davitt, the leader of the Land League. This organisation was fighting for better treatment for the tenants, because in Ireland

13

much of the land was part of huge estates, owned by landlords. The tenants paid high rents to the landlords, many of whom didn't even live in Ireland. The final aim of the Land War was to have the estates of the landlords broken up and the land bought by its Irish tenants. The other great hero had been Charles Stewart Parnell, who wanted Irish people to have their own parliament in Dublin. But since he had fallen in love with a married lady and was in disgrace, there was less talk of him. Michael found all the talk about government acts and home rule a bit boring. It was total freedom from England that was needed, the freedom that the Young Irelanders and the Fenians had fought for!

He sat in the warmth and listened to the buzz of voices, and made up his own mind about the rights and wrongs of the arguments. Michael was determined he would grow up and do something to help Ireland stand up to English rule. Had there not been a time before the English, when things must have been so much better? When the Irish were not seen as stupid, lazy and dishonest? A time when the horrors of the Famine could not have occurred? His father had told him stories of the terrible misery of the years when the potato crops failed. Old Mr Burke was talking about the famine now.

'Them were dreadful times. We were lucky. Clonakilty wasn't the worst hit. But the people of Skibbereen were in a terrible state. People, half-dead already, being thrown out of their houses because they couldn't pay the rent. You could see bodies on the ground with green marks around their mouths where they had tried to eat grass. And at the same time wheat and meat and all sorts of food was being shipped out of the country. So the landlords could buy more horses, and stuff themselves sick at big feasts in London. When I think of the bodies being piled into the huge pits over at Abbeystrewry – they hadn't the strength to bury them decently … there were no coffins, just cloth bags.'

Michael shuddered. He knew how important it was to send the dead off in a decent way. He had been only six when Dadda had died, but he still remembered his father's wake. The house packed with people. The mourners around the coffin, chanting decade after decade of the rosary, each person taking a turn to lead the prayer. The smell of the tall white candles. His brothers and sisters in tears. His mother, unable to sit down for even a moment. Rushing around, making sure everyone had enough to eat and drink, refilling glasses and cutting bread and bacon as if her life depended on it, loading the fire with turf against the bitter March weather.

There had been great sadness in the house. But there had also been singing and stories, and memories shared of a life lived well. It was horrible to think that thousands of people had not had that respect given to them when they died. Their families had been so desperate to find food for themselves that they had not even covered the faces of their beloved dead.

Many of those who had died had been children. Death was surely not quite so sad when the person who died had lived a long life. Michael's father had been an old, old man when he died. He had already been an old man when Michael, the youngest of eight children, was born. But Dadda had still been big and strong and still worked the farm. Michael remembered little things about him – the stories he had told, a kind voice, a presence that always made him feel totally safe. Some of the memories were a little fuzzy. Some of his memories might even have been stories told to him by his older brothers and sisters. Did he really remember deciding to go and dig potatoes when he was three? Or falling through the open trapdoor from the loft?

Michael jumped as Jimmy's great hammer came down onto a horseshoe with a loud clang. Sparks flew out and he realised that if he didn't get moving he would be in even more trouble than he was already.

'Are you off, Michael? I hope you won't get a scolding at home. I heard you were wrestling with the big boys again!'

'Everyone in this place hears everything!' said Michael indignantly.

'You're right there,' said Jimmy. 'That's the way it is in this country; the walls have ears.'

Michael couldn't help laughing as he imagined ears sticking out of walls. Jimmy laughed too, but added: ''Tis all very well, but even if you are a great wrestler for your age, you can't take on the world, young fella.'

Here we go again, thought Michael.

'Why can't I?' he asked.

'Well, you are only a little fella yet."

'I am not,' said Michael indignantly. 'I'm a big fella!'

The Storyteller

The lane was full of swirling leaves and the fields that stretched behind the bare hedges were brown and dull. A cart passed and splashed Michael with muddy water. He waved at the little donkey that was pulling it, and the donkey flicked his ears at him in a friendly fashion. At least the rain had stopped. Michael didn't mind the weather. What else would you expect at the end of October? He liked the swirling leaves, and he quite liked October too. His birthday was in October and there was always some kind of celebration on the day.

Whenever he walked home alone, he had special rituals. He had to say hello to the goats in Brennan's field; he had to salute the fairy fort and the lone hawthorn; he had to keep an eye out for any interesting birds or animals. His father had talked to him a lot about animals; he had been the seventh son of a seventh son and had the gift of healing them. He had been able to soothe any animal he laid his hands on, even their frisky white pony, Gypsy. His mother was always a little nervous around horses and ponies. Her mother had been thrown out of a trap and had never really recovered from it. Not that his mother would ever talk about her fear; she never admitted to being afraid of anything.

The house was coming into view. He felt his chest fill with pride when he saw it: two storeys, a solid red door and five windows, facing into wind and rain and standing safe and solid as a rock. After his father died, his mother had decided they needed a new and bigger house. Michael had been fascinated to see the walls of the house rise, the roof go on. He had wanted to be part of the adventure, and throughout the summer had stuck like a burr to the men working on the building, getting underfoot while trying to be helpful. But now the house was finished. The little stone cottage where all the children had been born was used as a house for the hens and ducks. There was even a flower garden. Nobody else in Woodfield had one. At the moment it wasn't very impressive, with nothing more than some late and very straggly chrysanthemums still bloom-ing there. But in the summer it was glorious, filled with scent and colour. His mother loved flowers.

He stopped and narrowed his eyes. The front door was open and he could see his mother there, talking to someone. Michael immediately felt more cheerful, for he recognised the worn green coat and wild white hair of Seánie of the Roads. Seánie was one of the travelling people. He sold bits of things, pins and needles and ribbons, but his main trade was in sto-ries. He could tell a tale like no-one else could. There were

19

many travellers like that, and they always came to Mrs Collins, who was famous for her hospitality. They were never refused a meal and a bed beside the fire in the kitchen. With a bit of luck, Seánie's arrival would divert his mother from his own misdeeds. Michael ran the last stretch home, where he was greeted by a welcome sea of barks and wagging tails from the farm dogs.

* * *

'Michael, move over there and let Lena closer to the fire, so she can see what it is she's reading. We don't want her eyes ruined.'

Michael shifted, dislodging the dog who gave half a growl and then licked his hand. His mother settled into her chair and took up her mending. Michael leaned in against the comforting warmth of her woollen skirt. There was always mending waiting for his mother in the evening. Michael himself was the biggest producer of torn trousers and worn-out socks.

His mother's hands were always busy, on the farm or in the house. She never stayed still, despite her slight limp. She made sure that every one of the family worked hard too. Nobody dared complain when they were given a job to do. Michael's mother's way of looking at things was that moaning about how tough things were was a waste of time. You just got on with the work.

And on the farm, there was always work. There was always something to be done. Bread to be baked; bacon to be cured, black and white puddings and sausages to be made. Butter to be churned. Chickens and geese and ducks to be fed. Cows to be milked. Pans to be scoured. Water to be fetched from the well. Crops to be sown and crops to be harvested; hay to be cut. Sallies to be cut too, and brought home to be made into baskets. Potatoes to be planted. Potatoes to be dug. Potatoes to be cleaned and cooked. Pots to be washed. Turf to be cut and brought into the house for the fire. Fires to be lit and ashes to be cleared. Sheets to be washed. Linen to be ironed. Beds to be made and furniture to be dusted.

Scoldings to be given. Scoldings to be endured.

Earlier, he had been given his scolding. Luckily his mother had been too busy to go on for long.

'Michael, you know very well you shouldn't have taken that cloak. You will have to stop being so thoughtless—'

Gentle Lena, as usual, tried to defend her little brother.

'Sure he was only having an adventure!'

'He never stops having adventures. And they always end up as trouble! Only last week I had to rescue my best bonnet, when he decided to put it on the pony!'

Michael couldn't help grinning. Gypsy had looked hilarious in the bonnet. But this brought on more scolding.

'Take that smile off your face, Michael Collins. You are old enough now to have a bit more sense – and to stop wrestling with the young fellas in your class, half of them twice your size.'

Seánie of the Roads looked up from the plate of bread and bacon he had been eating by the fireside.

'He's a healthy lad, with a heap of energy, Mrs Collins, and you should be glad he is so.'

His mother shrugged, then gave Michael a quick hug. 'Well, if I hear about any more fights at school, one of those willow canes you cut me yesterday won't be going into a basket; I'm warning you – it'll be put to good use for something else! But get on there, it's time to bring the cows in for milking. Katie, you go with him.'

The cows had been brought in and milked. The chickens and ducks had been fed, the pony stabled, everything made tight and secure. Then there was the evening meal, after which the washing up was done and the bread for tomorrow left to rise. After that there had been the rosary, and prayers said for his father's soul and for the health of family and friends.

Now, finally, the bustle of the day was over and there were other things to be done. Songs to be sung. Stories to be told. Everyone in the house, and some of the neighbours who had come in to hear Seánie, gathered around the fire. Michael and Patrick were weaving baskets out of the willow wands. Katie was darning a pair of stockings. His mother sewed, mending the tear that Michael had made, handling the great black cloak lovingly; it had belonged to her grandmother and would be passed down to the next generation.

There were gaps around the fireside. Hannie, Michael's oldest sister, had a job in the Post Office and lived in London now. The family saw her only during the summer holidays. Michael missed her; she always had time to listen to her little brother. Mary had been sent to school in Glasgow – she was going to become a teacher, like her sister Margaret. Johnnie would have the farm, but everyone else would have to make their own way in the world.

Johnnie was Michael's hero. Tonight, Margaret and Johnnie had gone out on their bicycles to their cousins down at Sam's Cross, with strict instructions from their mother not to be home too late. It was close to Halloween, the dark time of the year, a time when unquiet spirits and the fairies were out. Though Mary Ann Collins was a practical woman, like all of her neighbours, she was not going to take any risks with the Good People.

Lena was the only one not involved in darning or sewing or weaving. She sat in the inglenook seat, her head buried in a book. Lena was going away soon too. She was going to become a nun. She wasn't as strong as the others. She had almost died when she was small, badly burnt in an accident and only saved by her father's quick thinking and the help of the local Protestant clergyman. Lena was hoping to take the name Sister Mary Celestine. She had told Michael the reason why she was going to ask to take that name. Michael loved

23

the story, because it had his Dadda in it. Every story about his father was precious.

'One winter evening, there was just the two of us bringing the cows in for milking. All the stars were coming out. And we saw something bright flying across the sky. It was a shooting star,' she said. 'And Dadda said to me:

"Lena, I don't know much about anything...."

'I said: "Of course you do, Dadda. You know loads of things. Even Greek and Latin!"

'And he laughed and said: "Ah, only bits and pieces from the old hedge schoolmaster. That was all the education we got in those days. But listen to me; I do know something. I know something about God that you won't be told by the priest on a Sunday. God is what I see up there in those beautiful stars and in the evening sky. You can do a lot of praying, Helena, but you won't get much closer to God than when you are looking at his stars."

'And then he started to tell me all the names of the constellations. And all the Greek stories about the heroes and gods and goddesses. So, because Celeste means from Heaven, that's the name I would like to take. I want to be Sister Celestine.'

Michael had been impressed by the story, but he was less impressed with the life Lena was going to lead. She wouldn't be allowed home to see the farm and the family. She would be shut up for the rest of her life. It was one of the most horrible things that could happen to you, thought Michael, to be shut up somewhere and not allowed to go where you wanted, when you wanted. Now he whispered to Patrick:

'Do you ever feel as if being stuck somewhere, not able to get out, must be the very, very worst thing that can happen? Like when you're stuck in school and it's still hours to go before you can go home? Or...' He lowered his voice to make sure no-one else heard. 'During mass when the priest is going on and on in Latin?'

Patrick nodded.

'That's how I feel here most of the time, Michael. But I have my own plans – I am going to get away from all this. I'll get to America and work in a big city! Away from the cows and the mud and the rain—'

America! That was the place where thousands of Irish people had gone to after the Famine. America had saved the lives of countless Irish people. But it was so far away. When people went to America, they never came back. If Patrick left, Michael would never see his brother again.

He had no time to ask Patrick more about his plans. Their mother shushed them, for the storyteller had begun. It was a tale of one of the great heroes of Ireland's past, Fionn Mac Cool. This was Seánie's second start, for he had begun the story in Irish, forgetting that the Collins children had never learned to speak the language. Michael's parents had spoken Irish to each other, using it when they didn't want the children to understand what they were saying. His mother still sometimes sang in Irish to the cows when she milked them, because she said they gave sweeter milk. But the children were not allowed to speak it. English was the language you needed to get ahead in Ireland. Not just because it was the language of Britain, but because it was the language of America, the land of opportunity.

Michael forgot his work, engrossed in the tale the storyteller was weaving. Seánie's voice was soft in the darkness, closer to music than to ordinary speech. Some of the neighbours made an occasional comment as the tale was told, exclaiming at the wonders of the story and encouraging the storyteller. They were mostly old people. There were not many children of Michael's age living in Woodfield, but he didn't mind. He loved to listen to the quiet voices of the old people in the dark, to feel the warmth of the fire and breathe in the comforting smell of turf smoke and watch the flames of the fire flicker and fade. He could feel his eyes beginning to close as he got sleepier and sleepier. Then the neighbours began their own stories, tales of local fairies, like Cliona, who lived in the huge rock with the chimney and half-door, just outside Clonakilty.

'Doesn't she come out sometimes and snatch young men and boys and take them inside to live with her in her fairy palace? Be careful when you pass Cliona's rock or when you see her three magic birds. It's said that once she loved a mortal man, a young man who was lost when a great wave came in from the sea and pulled him away from her.'

Michael's mind drifted away into thoughts of the fairy woman. When he paid attention again, one of the neighbours had moved on to a story about the highwayman, Sam Wallace. He had robbed the rich to help the poor. His adventures were famous. The local crossroads, Sam's Cross, was called after him.

All the stories, all the heroes and fairy women, were getting mixed up in Michael's sleepy brain. Cliona was riding Sam Wallace's horse. The horse looked like Gypsy and then turned into a bicycle. That was one of Michael's dreams – to have his own bicycle. Then, in the dream, the bicycle was washed away in a great purple wave. Fionn McCool was in a prison cell with the moonlight coming through the window, and a voice was calling him to come and take his pike up for the battle. There were men marching to war ... and then there was a field of wheat being cut by a giant reaping machine. And then there was a voice singing in Irish, a song he could not understand but that made him want to cry with longing. *I want to be part of it*, thought Michael. *I want to be part of the song, part of the story.* He forced his eyes open and a waft of turf smoke came drifting towards him. He tried to blink the smoke out of his eyes. When he closed his eyes, though, he found he could not open them again. He was asleep.

A sod of turf shifted and sparked, fell, and within a moment the flame was snuffed out.

27

London, 1906

'Euston! Euston Station! This train is now arriving at Euston Station! All change!'

Screeching brakes, ear-piercing whistles. All change was right, thought Michael. London was a very big change from Woodfield. The noise of roaring engines was deafening, and the smell was so strong it felt as if it was roaring too. There seemed to be hundreds of people on the platform, all of them in a terrible rush and all of them strangers. The porters were bustling around, shouting offers to help with luggage. Their accents sounded harsh to Michael and they didn't offer to help him. They probably knew by looking at him that he didn't have the money to tip them. Anyway, he would have refused help if they had offered. Why would he need it, tall and strong as he was, and carrying only a single small case? The case that he had carefully guarded all the way from West Cork. It contained not much more than his best suit and some black and white pudding, sent as a present for Hannie. He hoped it would still be good to eat after the long journey!

Even if his case had been a big one, he couldn't have asked for help from the porters. He had no idea how much to tip them and he knew he had to be very careful with his money. All through the journey he had kept it close to him, along with his precious letter telling him that he had been successful in the Civil Service exams and should present himself at the West Kensington Post Office to take up a position as Boy Clerk.

Everything was strange and although he could hardly admit it even to himself, everything was a little frightening. He was tired and anxious. He had been so excited about making the trip to London. Now he was exhausted. He had been looking forward to leaving home for ages but it had been very hard when the time finally arrived. There had been the sadness of leaving his mother and the farm. He had gone around all the animals and said goodbye, trying not to cry when he gave Gypsy a last hug. Gypsy had looked sadly at him, her eyes cloudy now. He was almost sure that when he came back for his holidays in the summer, she would be gone. As he climbed into the trap, he remembered running after Lena when she went away to the convent, where she had got her wish and become Sr Celestine. Now it was his turn to look back and wave to the little crowd gathered at the farmhouse door.

From Cork, he had taken the train to Kingsbridge. It was his first time in Dublin. That city had been huge and frightening too, and the streets were so full of poor people and rough-looking men that he was glad not to be staying there.

Then there was the slow trek across the Irish Sea and the even slower journey up the river to Liverpool. The voyage had been rough but he had followed the advice of one of the lads he had met on the boat. The boy was older than Michael and had made the journey many times:

'If you feel sick, find a place to stretch out flat, close your eyes and wait until it's all over. It'll be boring as Hell, but at least you won't end up feeding the fishes your breakfast!'

He had not been sick, but he had felt really awful by the time the boat had docked. He had panicked slightly about finding the railway station and the right train, but he kept telling himself that lots and lots of people had done this journey before him. Patrick had been only a couple of years older than he was when he left for America. Now that was some journey! And Patrick had travelled with no-one to meet him when he arrived. He would have Hannie waiting for him.

He looked around the platform. Men in business suits and bowler hats, ladies in elegant dresses, some of them wearing furs. Everyone looked as if they knew where they were going and what they were doing. Everyone except him. But there, waving frantically and with a smile that lit up her face, was Hannie. He struggled through the crowd and when he reached her, she hugged him tight.

'Well, you made it! We will have to send a wire to let Mam know. But let's get you home. You must be worn out.'

Hannie was tall, with bright eyes and a slightly beaky nose. She was dressed in clothes that were much more stylish than anything Michael had ever seen. No heavy black cloaks for her! Michael realised that even though she was his sister, he didn't really know Hannie very well. She had left home for London when he was small, so the only times he had met her were when she came home for her holidays. But it was such a relief to hear someone speak in a soft west Cork voice!

As she walked briskly along beside him, her movements and gestures reminded him of his mother. She led him from the station out into the teeming mass that was London, making her way confidently through the crowds. Tall red omnibuses, carts and carriages and motors jostled with drays and bicycles for room in the streets. Most of the streets were wider than the market squares at home and even the pavements were wider than the streets of Clonakilty. Wide as they were, they were still packed with people, all of them pushing and rushing. The air was thick with smells that Michael didn't recognise. There was a yellowish tinge to it and it made him cough as he walked along. Hannie said very little until they reached what seemed to be another railway station. They went down the steep steps and Michael realised that they would be travelling underground.

His jaw dropped.

'It's amazing, isn't it?' said Hannie. 'It's an underground train.

It will take us all the way to Shepherd's Bush, without having to stop for any traffic.'

They made their way through a maze of passages lit by harsh lights, until they came to a platform. Within moments, a train came barrelling towards them, shrieking its arrival. It was packed, and they were lucky to find seats side by side, with Michael clutching his suitcase on his lap. Hannie finally took the time to study her brother closely.

'I swear, every time I see you, you have grown another few inches. You have become a young man, and you only fifteen!' Michael didn't know what to say to this, so he just grinned. Hannie continued, 'How is everyone at home?' Michael shrugged. Hannie knew as well as he did that their mother had not been well for months. It didn't stop her working herself to the bone, though, and refusing help from everyone.

'Mam is a bit tired, but she refuses to go to the doctor. She says once the spring comes again, she'll be fine. Everyone else is great. Oh, poor old Gypsy is not too good. Getting on. They all send their love.'

'Gypsy too?' Hannie laughed. 'And how are Margaret and Denis?'

'They are grand, and the children are all grand too.'

Michael had stayed with his sister Margaret and her husband in Clonakilty while he studied for the Civil Service exams. While he was there, he had spent a lot of time with his best friend, Jack Hurley. Jack was coming over to London later in the year, and he couldn't wait to see him. Jack's sister Kathy was married to Michael's brother Johnnie, so they could describe each other as kind of cousins.

As if she had read his thoughts, Hannie said, 'You must be looking forward to Jack coming over. And Nancy too; did you hear cousin Nancy has got a job in the Post Office? Half of west Cork will be over here with you! But be careful, Michael. If I have one bit of advice for you, it's this. Don't spend all your time with people from home. I have seen some people do that and they get nowhere. Make the most of the chances you will get here. This is one of the great cities of the world and there is so much to do! I love it here; I'm not sure that I could ever go back home now.' She paused before continuing. 'I'm going to bring you to Madame Tussaud's and the Tower of London, to Kensington Gardens, to loads of places. There's so much happening – plays and music and libraries and museums and associations to join. I'll bring you to a play next weekend. Do you like the theatre?'

Michael shrugged again. He was too embarrassed to admit that he had never been to a play. Hannie smiled. 'I am sure you will love it! What is it that you like to do at home?'

'Well, I spend a lot of time going cycling with Jack – you know, he likes to be called Seán now. I do a lot of sports. I play hurling and Gaelic football, and I do running and athletics too.'

33

'You will have plenty of chances to do all that here; there are lots of places to train – the Olympics were held here this year! And the GAA has a London branch. What about other games?'

'I won't go near soccer or rugby! They're the games the English use to brainwash us! To try to get us to think that we are part of their culture!'

Hannie sighed and looked around to make sure that nobody was listening. Michael was going to have to learn to keep some of these opinions to himself, especially in public places like this. Her mother had asked her to try to get Michael away from the dangerous, revolutionary ideas he had developed over the last couple of years. According to her, Michael and Jack Hurley had spent hours discussing how Ireland could be freed from British rule. Michael was bright – top of his class – but she was afraid that there was a reckless side to him. All that energy might – as she had whispered to Hannie in a very private conversation in the cowshed during Hannie's last visit home – just might get him into trouble.

Keeping Michael out of trouble was going to be no joke, Hannie thought. He was tall and strong-looking, with a wild head of black hair and grey eyes that held a spark of what could only be described as devilment. Sport will help, she thought, lots of racing around and kicking balls. She thought of the peaceful life she had led for the past few years; her pleasant English friends, her kind landlord who had obligingly made another room available for Michael in his quiet house. Things were going to change, that was for sure. She sighed. Then she smiled at her brother. After all, she was very fond of him.

'All that sport is going to keep you hungry. The good news is that we live just over a bakery!'

'Are English cakes the same as Irish ones?' Michael asked.

Hannie laughed. 'They are indeed, most of them. And the ones that are different are just as good!'

* * *

Things were indeed very different for both Hannie and Michael after Michael moved to London. Michael struggled through his first weeks at the Post Office, a little bit over-whelmed by the size of the building and the number of people working there – nearly two thousand altogether. He had to get used to unfamiliar ways, to having every minute of his day watched and clocked, to listening to Cockney voices calling him Irish Mick. When they couldn't be bothered remember-ing his name, they just called him Paddy. In the beginning, it had made him angry. He came home one evening in a tearing temper.

Hannie took one look at him and said, 'Sit down there, Michael, and tell me what the trouble is.'

Michael shook his head but sat down. He was so angry, he could hardly speak.

'How is it that every English person, no matter how thick they are, seems to think they are cleverer than every Irish person? That somehow because we don't speak like them and because we come from across the water we are not that bright? What makes them feel they can make stupid jokes about pigs in the parlour and potatoes for breakfast and dinner and tea? That they can copy our accent as a joke and sometimes not even bother to remember our names?'

'You know that's not the case, Michael,' Hannie said quietly. 'Look at our landlord, Mr Lawrence; look at all my friends who are never anything but kind to you. They certainly don't think you are stupid. I know it's hard for you to listen to all the mockery, but it's just people being lazy and ignorant. Maybe it's because of their Empire; some English people laugh at French people and Italians and Jews, and lots of other nations too, you know. It's the way it is. It's what nearly every Irish person in London has to put up with.'

Michael pushed back his chair, scraping it fiercely against the floor. 'I know, Hannie,' he said. 'I know, but it's not right that we should have to put up with it and it really makes me angry. Does it not make you angry too?'

Hannie shrugged. 'Sometimes it still does,' she said. 'But I won't give those people the satisfaction of knowing they have annoyed me. They are just ignoramuses who are trying to make themselves feel more important by putting other people down. Don't let them get to you, Michael. And remember what Mam always said: Don't waste time complaining. Just get on with the work.'

So Michael tried to take Hannie's advice. And he found that most of the time it worked. He still sometimes got angry but he learned to respond to the smart comments with a joke and a smile, and he realised that Hannie was right. Most English people were just ordinary people, nice people, trying to get through their days as best they could, not really interested in where someone was from, only in whether they worked well and were pleasant to talk to.

As the months went by, he became more settled. Jack – who he was still getting used to calling Seán – had come over, and he spent a lot of time with him and with his cousin, Nancy. He was meeting new people, making new friends, most of them young Irish people. The work – mostly addressing envelopes or writing out the same sentences about loans and deposits – was no problem to him. In fact, it was boring. Michael daydreamed that one day they would use typewriters to do all that boring writing, so that people like him would not have to spend seven hours a day, five-and-a-half days a week at it. In the end, he got really fast at his job and became one of the quickest workers in the office.

He made the most of what free time he had. There was the GAA, where he could work off the energy that built up inside him and sometimes made him feel as if he might explode. But there were always times when it felt as if the city was crushing him with the weight of its people and its buildings. At those times, he dreamt of the summer holidays, when he would be able to get back to Sam's Cross and see fields and trees instead of buildings; donkeys and ponies instead of trams and cars; and his mother and his family instead of streets full of strange faces.

Michael was thinking of his holidays one foggy April evening when he came in from work. As he entered the flat, he was surprised to see that Hannie was at home before him. She was sitting at the table by the window and she had something in her hands. He grinned at her. 'I thought you were planning on going to the library,' he said. 'But you're right to stay in. It's awful today – it's a real London pea-souper out there.'

He took off his cap and coat and bent to take off his boots, which were covered in mud from the foul weather. Hannie said nothing. She kept on folding and refolding the piece of paper in her hands as if she didn't know what to do with it. Michael looked up. He realised that something awful had happened. For one stupid moment he thought – it's Gypsy, she's dead. Then he realised it must be something far worse.

'It's Mam, isn't it?' he said. 'She's gone?'

Hannie nodded. She came over to where Michael was standing, half-way through taking off his left boot, too stunned even to finish the job. She put her arms around him and leant her head on his shoulder.

'Yes, she's left us. Oh Michael, I can't believe she has gone! Home will never be the same again!'

Winning

'It's a goal!' Michael roared with delight and punched the air. From his position in midfield, he could see that Seán had scored. The Geraldines just might win after all. It had been killing him to see how badly they were doing. Some of the players were useless. As Secretary of the club, he had no role in training, but if he had, he thought, he would knock some of their heads together. But it wasn't just that the Geraldines had losers on the team. The ref had made some very dodgy calls during this game. Michael firmly believed that this was because Peadar had it in for him. During the last few years, he had had more than one row with this particular referee.

'You're a mucker and a mullacker, Michael Collins,' Peadar had told him. 'Don't think I haven't seen you pulling jerseys and poking people in the ribs, and worse. When you get in close, you're like a young savage. I'm not letting you away with that kind of behaviour. It's not all about winning, you know!'

Michael just shrugged. He didn't care. He got in there and he did what he felt was needed to beat the hell out of the other team! He couldn't stand the idea of losing. He glanced down the field where things were looking dangerous again. If they were going to win this game, he had better get moving. A cold wind blew rain into his face, and the pitch was a mud bath. Michael raced forward and felt himself slip – he was down on his face in the sludge. He didn't care about that either. What mattered was that they were winning!

Years had passed since Michael had started work in London, and he had changed a great deal during that time. He had become big and tall, with broad shoulders. He had grown a moustache and quickly shaved it off after his cousin Nancy had burst out laughing at him when she saw it.

He knew London well now. He was as familiar with the latest plays and novels as Hannie was. He had worked in different jobs, and had discovered that he was a good organiser as well as being good with figures. He had also learned that he could work well with all kinds of different people. At one stage, he had thought he might make a career in the Civil Service and he had gone to night classes to prepare for the examinations. He had spent over three hours every evening, four days a week, going to those classes. But he hadn't done very well. In the essays he wrote, he had not been able to stop himself criticising England. In some cases, that had not gone down very well with the teachers.

As time went on, he became more and more involved in the Irish community in London and he spent less time at his classes. There were thousands of Irish people living in London and they had set up all sorts of groups. As well as being deeply involved in the GAA, Michael had taken Irish classes at the Gaelic League, the organisation set up to encourage people to learn the Irish language.

Hannie knew about the Geraldines and the Gaelic League. She even knew that her brother was a member of the Volunteers. Seán Hurley had enlisted him. The Volunteers drilled like soldiers, ready to defend Ireland if the promises of Home Rule were not kept. The British had promised the Irish their own parliament in Dublin, but that had been put on hold when the war with Germany broke out. What made things even more complicated was the fact that so many people in the north of Ireland didn't want Home Rule. In Belfast and the counties around it, people were afraid of being ruled by Dublin. They were proud of being part of the British Empire. These people, the Unionists, had been the first to set up an organisation that called itself the Volunteers, and they were very ready to fight against a parliament in Dublin.

Almost all the Ulster Volunteers went to fight in the British army in France and Belgium. Some of the Irish Volunteers went too; others refused to be part of the army of the British Empire. Michael had become very involved with this branch of the Volunteers. He drilled with them every week. Though she felt a little uneasy about it, Hannie did not try to stop Michael from being part of the Volunteers. What she did not know, though, was that her brother was also a member of the Irish Republican Brotherhood or IRB. This was a secret group that had been set up years before to fight for Irish independence. Michael had been sworn into this group by a GAA friend called Sam Maguire. Sam was from west Cork too.

Michael held long conversations with Seán and the other Volunteers about how Ireland could become independent from Britain. He didn't tell Hannie anything about these conversations, or about his most secret dreams of returning to Ireland and fighting for that freedom. Hannie still fretted over him, but she had realised long ago that she really did not have very much control over her younger brother. They still lived together and they still got along very well, but by now Michael had learned how to keep secrets, even from those closest to him.

Hannie and Michael looked like thousands of other Londoners, travelling to work in a city that was full of army uniforms. It was a city that was gradually also filling up with beggars sitting in doorways, their legs or arms or eyes, or sometimes their minds, gone. Michael often got odd looks and hissed comments from people who thought that someone his age should be fighting in France or Belgium. He didn't say anything. He knew that he was not a coward; he just had a different war to fight!

After the match was over, Seán came over to him. 'Will you

be at Nancy's this evening?' he asked quietly. Michael nodded.

'Well, can we make sure to leave together? I have something I want to talk to you about.'

'Are you not walking Kathleen home?' Michael loved to tease Seán about the girl he was sort of, kind of, going out with.

'She's not coming tonight.'

'I'll go along with you so.'

'You'd better get yourself cleaned up first – were you rolling in the mud?'

* * *

There was a large group of people crowded into Nancy's small flat. She shared it with Susan, a girl from Clare that Michael had begun to spend a lot of time with. The girls were fun. They loved dancing and singing and music. They also shared Michael and Seán's ideas about freedom for Ireland. Among the young Irish people in London, there was a feeling that this was a special time. Plays and poetry were pouring out of Ireland. Ordinary people were discovering their wonderful traditions of music and literature. Ireland was a country to be proud of.

There was a great deal of laughing and talking in the flat, in accents from all over the country. The rain had stopped and all the sash windows had been pushed open. The girls sat on the ledges, leaning out to catch the last of the brightness, and admiring the yellow pears on the fruit trees, wet and shining in the September light. The girls were still wearing their summer dresses, refusing to admit that it was almost autumn and they had months of icy winds and yellow fogs to look forward to. Their clothes had changed from the delicate colours, the laces and muslins that had impressed Michael when he first arrived in London. Now they were much more practical. The skirts were shorter and made of heavier material. Times had changed. Women now worked in jobs that had been seen as men's work a few years before. They had to – the young men were away fighting. Like the Irish, the women had received promises about what would happen when the war was over. They had been promised the right to vote!

The big news of the night was that Ted Brierty was headed for America. He stood chatting to Michael and Seán, half excited, half nervous.

'I have an offer of a job over there, in Chicago. Isn't that where your brother is, Michael?'

Michael nodded. 'I haven't heard much from him lately. He offered to pay for me to go over to him but I didn't take him up on it.'

Michael sometimes wondered if he had made the right choice. Here in London, he would never really be anything more than Irish Mick, no matter how many classes he took or examinations he passed. And by staying here he ran the risk

45

of being forced into joining the army. He was working in an American company now and it would be easy enough to get a transfer. If he went to America, he could not be conscripted. But he was still not ready to give up on his idea of fighting for Ireland.

Nancy interrupted them, catching Michael's arm to get his attention.

'Our branch of the Gaelic League is thinking of putting on a performance of *The Countess Kathleen*. What do you say, Michael – do you want to try out for a part in it?'

'I can do a lot for Ireland, Nancy, but I am sorry to say that I can't act!'

Nancy laughed. 'No, nor sing either!'

'Are you a real Irishman at all?' mocked Susan, coming over to join them, with a smile on her face.

Michael smiled back. Susan was serious and kind and he loved to make her laugh despite herself. If it had been Seán teasing him, Michael would have taken a dive at him and wrestled him to the ground. Now he just said, 'Well, I can dance anyway. Are you two going to the céilí on Friday night?'

Susan nodded. 'Wouldn't miss it for the world. I'll see you there?'

'Of course you will!'

But Michael didn't make it to the céilí. By Friday, he had taken leave from his job and had made his way over to Dublin.

Seán had given him some news, whispered quietly when they sat together in the snug in the Shamrock Bar later that evening.

'You've heard the rumours, haven't you, Mick?'

Michael gave an impatient sigh. 'I have. But we've been listening to rumours for years and nothing has been happening! This war will be ended before we know it and we will have lost our chance to take a hit at England while their attention is on other things!'

Seán laughed. 'This war will be going on for another while yet. There are too many people making money out of it for it to be otherwise. Wasn't it supposed to be over in a few months? By Christmas, they said. It's already been going on over a year, and there's worse to come, I'm sure of it. But listen, I want you to come over to Ireland with me, so we can train there. There's a whole army of Volunteers being drilled in a place called Larkfield. It's in Kimmage, near Dublin, and it's owned by Joe Plunkett's family. We can drill there together and be ready to go if something does happen. And the signs are there will be something moving early in the New Year.'

'But half the Volunteers won't come out to fight, or have already enlisted and gone off to war! I'm starting to think it might be a good idea to get away myself, maybe over to America. Here, I'll never get any further, and I don't want to either, to get stuck in some poky little house with no freedom and no fresh air. What I wouldn't give sometimes, to be off riding my bike in the lanes of west Cork with you and Katie!'

'You still really miss home, don't you, Mick?'

'I do. Even with my mother gone, I always feel happy when I am at Woodfield. I miss Ireland so much. Do you know what I saw the other evening, Seán, when I was out with a gang of lads from home? It was right in the heart of the city. I couldn't believe my eyes. Out of a laneway comes a chap with a cart, and a little donkey pulling it. The donkey was for all the world like the ones at home, just making its way along the noisy, dirty street with its ears up, going so patiently, so quietly through the city. We all cheered him! And I thought to myself, that's what I want to fight for. For the ordinary people going about their business on the small, quiet roads of home. But it looks like I'm never going to get the chance.'

'Don't give up yet! Go to Dublin, Michael. Talk to people like Tom Clarke and Seán Mac Diarmada. They'll be able to give you more news than I can. I'm dying to hear what you think of old Tom — and what Tom thinks of you!'

* * *

Tom Clarke looked at Michael over his glasses and shook his head. This impatient young man had a long way to go. Tom had spent years in English jails and he had learned patience the hard way. He was sitting behind the counter of the tobacconist shop he ran in the centre of Dublin, while his wife Kathleen bustled about behind Michael, arranging things in the window and at the same time keeping an eye out in case any soldiers or policemen were approaching. He echoed Seán's words:

'Don't give up, Michael. Come back over to us – you'll find a job easily enough – and make ready with us. I'm telling you, the wheels have started turning. By the end of next year, we might well be living in an Irish republic!'

* * *

On a cold day at the end of November, Hannie sat where she always sat, by the big bay window where she could catch the light for work or reading. But the room she was sitting in was more comfortable and this was a much bigger, brighter flat than the little space they had shared so many years ago. She was knitting and she glared at Michael over her glasses when he flung his hat across the room and came bounding towards her.

'Don't you dare!'

Michael grinned and made a dive for the knitting. He thought it hilarious to pull the needles out – he called it a gesture against the war, but Hannie called it pure mischief. Hannie was knitting socks for the soldiers at the front. She pulled her knitting onto her lap and looked at him sternly. She was older and a little grey now, but still as anxious and as kind as ever.

'Michael, I know by your face you have something to tell me. And I know what you are going to say. You are going to go back to Dublin, aren't you, to get mixed up in the Lord knows what over there? That's what that little trip a couple months ago was about, isn't it?'

'Hannie, it's time. It's going to be such a big adventure, as Peter Pan would say!' Michael smiled and Hannie couldn't help but smile back.

'You and your big adventures! Remember when we went to see the pantomime, just after you came over? You were bowled over. And then we went to see the statue of Peter Pan in Kensington Gardens. But Michael, it's death that Peter Pan is talking about, when he talks about an awfully big adventure.'

Her face became very serious. 'I am worried about all these plans you have. I worry about who and what you are involved with. I worry that you might well be going to your death. God knows, I tried hard enough through the years to keep you safe. I promised Mam—'

'I'll never forget all you've done for me, Hannie. I will always be thankful for how you helped me during that awful time after Mam died.'

Michael felt a lump in his throat as he said it. The pain was still there, although not so overpowering now. He remembered the first, dreadful months, the days of suddenly realising that he would never see his mother's face again or hear her

50

singing to the cows. He would never wrap his arms around her and let her black cloak fall around him so that he felt protected from the world. It had been so hard, but Hannie had been there, always ready with a word of comfort or a hug. Now he wanted to give *her* the hug, but she was looking stern and worried, so he said, 'Will you be able to keep on the flat? I'll send some money over if you need it. I know that you really like it here.'

As he said this, he wondered where he would get money to send. He didn't even have a job sorted out, and if the rebellion happened, he might never have one again. *But if I talk about things like this, I won't start to cry*, he said to himself. Being practical had saved him from tears a great many times. Thinking about what had to be done instead of letting his feelings take over.

Hannie was crying now. 'I'll be grand,' she said. 'Don't worry about me. But as for you: I don't know what you are going into, Michael, but I know it's trouble. You have that bee in your bonnet about fighting for freedom and there's nothing going to take it out of you. But listen to me for a couple of minutes. All I am asking is that you please, please, please be careful. And I don't just mean if you are rushing off into a fight, I mean even with the people that are on your own side. You still have an awful temper and it can make you enemies, you know! You can rub people up the wrong way. You know your history better than I do. You know all the stories of betrayals to the English by our own people. They could betray you too, Michael. You could end up on some lonely gallows, with the ballad-singers in the streets making up songs about you ... and I don't want you to be part of some sad song or story! I want you to live and have a long, happy life! I'd rather have a living brother than a brother who goes down in the history books as a hero, a dead hero!'

Michael laughed.

'Nothing and no-one is going to kill me, Hannie. This time, things will be different! This time, we will make sure that freedom really happens. I promise you, Hannie, my dear, I won't let any of them get me!'

Losing

*S*o this is it. This is the Rebellion. This is what I dreamed of for so many years. The glorious fight for freedom. This is a huge bloody mess.

Michael looked around him, trying his best not to hear the tuneless singing and the groans of the wounded men. He couldn't decide which noise was worse. He knew the men were singing to try to keep their spirits up, but the songs about victory and glory grated on his nerves. There was not much glory to be seen here in the General Post Office of Dublin in April 1916. Just total confusion and an awful lot of blood.

Men wandered about the large open halls of what was now the headquarters of the rebel army. No-one seemed very sure about what they were meant to be doing or where they were meant to be going. Many of the men were wounded and all were filthy, covered in smuts from the explosions and the firing. The smell of burning was everywhere. Burning buildings, burning metal and rubber. Sometimes burning flesh.

One young boy was kneeling in a corner, facing away from everyone, desperately reciting the rosary and clutching the beads, as if, Michael thought, that was going to save him

from the bombardment of shells and the spurts of gunfire outside. Commandant Pearse, their leader, drifted by, like a man
in a mist. Michael remembered Kathleen Clarke's analysis of
Pearse's ability to lead: 'He knows as much about commanding as my dog.' Michael thought she was right; Pearse couldn't
organise himself out of a paper bag.

*Maybe he wants to die. I don't. I want to get out of this sardine
can that is getting hotter by the minute. I want to live. I want to be
around to cut the cord with England for once and for all and then
rebuild this street and this city and this country. And if I do manage
to survive, that's exactly what I am going to do. Get on with the work
and finish the job.*

But just now he felt something that he had never expected
to feel in the middle of the long-awaited rebellion – ever so
slightly bored. They had all been hanging around, not doing
very much, for hours. Michael was in charge of a small group
of men, but his main jobs were in the Operations Room and
as aide-de-camp to Joseph Plunkett, one of the main leaders.
He had been in the GPO since Monday. This was Friday.

Monday had been a glorious day. With heads held high,
the rebel army had marched from Liberty Hall to the GPO.
Pearse had read the Proclamation of the Republic of Ireland
and Michael had felt his heart fill with pride. Finally it was
happening! Michael had been with Joe Plunkett, who had had
to stay in a hotel in Dublin the night before the Rising as he

was too weak to travel in from Larkfield. Joe was an amazing character. He was very ill from lung disease but he had been determined to take part in the Rising. He risked being executed, and even if he was just imprisoned, it was clear that he would die if he was put into one of Dublin's cold, damp jails.

Even during that march, there was a small voice in Michael's head, asking him if the Rising was already a lost cause. The lead-up to Monday had been a disaster. The Rising had been planned, then cancelled. Then the decision had been made to go ahead. The first plan had been to have uprisings all over the country. Then the news came that the arms that were needed by the rebels had been lost. The ship carrying German arms had been scuppered on the Kerry coast. The plan was changed. The Rising would happen only in Dublin. James Connolly, the leader of the Irish Citizen Army, an army made up of workers, explained to Michael why they had decided to go ahead:

'We don't have a choice. If we wait, it will be the end of us. The army is planning a huge round-up of anyone suspected of plotting against the Crown. The Castle has an amazing spy network. It seems to know what we are planning to do before we know ourselves!'

Michael wondered if he would have been one of the people arrested. He had come to Dublin in January, with Seán and some of the other lads who had been Volunteers or IRB members in London. He had got a job working in a stockbroker's office, but he also worked for the Plunkett family. Officially he was meant to be a sort of secretary to Count Plunkett, Joe Plunkett's father. But he had spent most of his time drilling and making bombs out at Larkfield. It had been very exciting. More exciting than all this waiting around, he thought.

Most of the action he had seen was trying to stop looters from going on the rampage among the fancy shops of O'Connell Street. The poor people of Dublin, barefoot and starving, had gone crazy. They had broken the windows of the shops and had forced their way through those windows, kicking and pushing and shouting, into a world of food and luxury they had only ever dreamed of. Seán MacDiarmada, one of the leaders, had tried his best to stop them. He had tears in his eyes when they laughed at him, this young man stooped over a stick, roaring at them to respect the new Republic. It had been a long way from what any of the Volunteers had imagined when they had dreamed of declaring a Republic, when they had listened to Pearse's inspiring speeches.

But Seán Mac Diarmada was an idealist. Michael looked around at the men who were leading the Rising. All of them were on fire with high ideals, with courage, with patriotism. If sincerity and courage were all that were needed for victory, you would follow them all to Hell and back. MacDiarmada was a poet. His face glowed when he spoke about his dream of an independent Irish nation.

James Connolly's dream was slightly different; it was of a republic for the working people. A republic where the country's resources were shared equally among everyone who lived in it. A republic with no ragged, barefoot children, living ten to a room with no food and no heat, dying by the dozen of diseases caused by poverty. Tom Clarke was there too, his face lit up with joy that he was being given the chance to fight once more for his dream. Neither Tom nor Joe spoke very much about definite plans for the future. *If we do get a republic,* thought Michael, *will anyone know what to do with it?*

Michael was weary to the bone but he knew better than to let his men see it. He moved over towards one of the huddles and tried to sing along with them. It was hard to keep up the front. He knew that his temper could get the better of him and he was determined not to let it happen during this time. If he ended up dead, he wanted to be remembered as a disciplined soldier, as a dignified Collins from west Cork. As someone his mother and father would have been proud of. Even Hannie would have to say that he died a noble death.

But he would really, really prefer not to have to die at all …

Pearse was calling the officers over to where he had been deep in conversation with James Connolly. Connolly was lying on a stretcher, his arm in a sling, his bandaged leg stretched out in front of him. He was badly wounded – he had been shot in the arm, and his ankle was also shattered. The nurses were worried that there were signs of gangrene in his leg, which could kill him if it was left unattended. He was in great pain, but he growled a Scottish curse or two at Winnie, one of the nurses, who was trying to make him rest a little.

'Stop your fussing, woman! Sure look at me. A morning in bed, a good book to read, and an insurrection all at the same time. It's revolution *de luxe*!'

Michael gave a snort of laughter but Pearse didn't smile. He didn't have much of a sense of humour. Winnie didn't laugh either, and she said nothing. She was one of the Cumann na mBan women who were part of the garrison. They were the women's branch of the Volunteers and had been very active in the Rising. They had worked mainly as despatchers, bringing food and messages to the other rebel outposts in the city. They had also been kept busy nursing the wounded. Very few of them had been involved in the fighting. Constance Markievicz was one of those who had fought. She was second in command in Michael Mallin's battalion, who had taken over St Stephen's Green.

Pearse looked around the little group and cleared his throat. He didn't look at all happy about whatever he was planning to say.

'We are going to have to evacuate,' he began. 'Since the *Helga* came up the Liffey, we haven't had a chance of holding on here. She is loaded with guns and fresh ammunition. We will need to move to Moore Street. You will exit the building in an orderly fashion, taking your men with you. Obviously we will be fired on as we leave.'

How can we exit in an orderly fashion and avoid getting shot at the same time? thought Michael. But he saluted and said nothing except, 'Yes sir.'

Pearse hadn't mentioned that the roof of the GPO was on fire and it was hotter than Hell in the building. If they stayed inside, they would no longer be sardines; they would end up as roast Easter lamb.

When Michael joined his men, his cousin Gearóid O'Sullivan, another Volunteer, had just come in from O'Connell Street. He asked Michael what he was smiling at. 'We're pulling out, heading for Moore Street. At least I won't be burnt alive in a post office. I'm haunted by post offices, all the way back! The Post Office was my first job in London!'

Thinking of that job made him think of Hannie. 'Gearóid,' he said. 'If anything happens me, you will be sure to go to her and let her know that this is how I would have wanted it, won't you? That I was happy to die fighting for Ireland.'

Gearóid nodded. 'I will,' he said. 'If I make it through this myself.'

There was silence for a moment. Gearóid tried to lighten things up by asking, 'Talking of post offices, what happened to that poor eejit of a soldier who came in to buy a stamp? He was in an awful state.'

Michael laughed. 'I told him we didn't shoot prisoners, but I don't think he believed me. He was shaking like a leaf!'

'What did you do with him?'

'I dumped him outside in the street. Told him to hail a taxi! He didn't laugh at my joke. I hope he got away all right. What's going on out there at the moment?'

Gearóid sighed. 'My latest mission was to try to stop two lads hauling a piano up to a tenement in Mountjoy Square. They didn't listen to me when I told them to halt and I was damned if I was going to shoot them!'

Michael laughed again. 'Well, I hope they enjoy knocking a few tunes out of it. Listen, we have to get moving. You'd better get your kit together.'

'So we're off to Moore Street. That's a bit of a comedown. The General Post Office to a fruit and veg market!'

As he led his troop out of the GPO and peered around the corner to see if there were any British soldiers in sight, Michael had the ridiculous thought that they were like a gang of school kids. Here they were, getting ready to race across to the other side of the schoolyard in some child's game. He remembered the dramatic falls to the ground he used to make when he had been 'shot' in those games. But in this game, if a shot rang out and someone fell to the ground, that soldier would be unlikely to get up again.

They made it to Moore Street and tried to snake along the street, but the fire was so heavy that they had to give up within minutes. They took shelter in a fishmonger's shop at Number 16. The smell of rotting fish in the shop was dreadful, but the rebels set up their new headquarters there, and set about tunnelling through the walls to get further down the street. Michael and some of his troop did a quick sortie out to the north of Moore Street, firing at the soldiers in the Rotunda Hospital gardens.

Late in the evening, a young Cumann na mBan member came rushing to the door, breathless and in shock. She brought some very bad news.

'The Four Courts has fallen – the brigade at Church Street couldn't hold them back any longer. There have been casualties—'

Michael pricked up his ears. That was where Seán was fighting.

'Any word on Jack Hurley?' He asked the young woman. The girl's face dropped.

'I'm sorry, sir; he was one of the men who got it. Very sorry to say so, sir.'

'It's not your fault!' growled Michael. He moved to a corner and sat hunched there, his face to the wall so that no-one could see the tears that he could not stop from falling. He couldn't believe it. Seán was dead. His crazy, laughing friend. He wouldn't hear Seán's mocking voice again, teasing him about his temper or his clumsiness. There would be no more wrestling matches or joshing about girlfriends. Seán had been his best friend since he was twelve and started school in Clonakilty; Seán had known when to talk to him and when to leave him to his own thoughts. They had spent countless evenings walking together through the dark streets of London, talking about the new Ireland they would build. Seán had been part of this great adventure, and now that he was gone, it seemed even less of an adventure and more of a nightmare.

Michael noticed that some of the men were looking at him strangely. *No more tears. Don't let them see how hard this is for you. Leaders have to remain calm and strong. But by God I'll make them pay for what they did to my friend. I'll make sure that Seán will not have died in vain. I'll carry on the fight for each one of the men who have died.*

The next day was Saturday. Pearse called the troops together and said quietly that the decision had been made to surrender.

'There have been too many lives lost already,' he said.

'I would rather die fighting!' growled Tom Clarke. There was a faint cheer from some of the men.

Pearse was quiet and dignified. Perhaps, thought Michael, he had always known that this was where the rebellion was leading.

'I am Commander-in-Chief, and these are my orders. Civilians are being killed – old people and children. We can't risk any more lives. Now, Nurse O'Farrell?' He called over Elizabeth, one of the Cumann na mBan members.

'Yes, sir?'

'I want you to bring this to General Maxwell. It's the surrender papers, signed by me. You will need a white flag and you will need to show a Red Cross badge in a prominent position. It's a dangerous task – I do not think the British will shoot at you but you could easily be hit by a stray bullet. Are you willing to do this?'

'Of course I am, sir!'

'Good. And as soon as that is done, we must start getting the news to the other battalions in the city. They must surrender too, as quickly as possible to avoid any more lives being lost. We will need women to go to Boland's Mills, where De Valera is, and to the Mendicity Institute and the College of Surgeons. And of course to the Union. God help us, I hope Ceannt is able to persuade Cathal Brugha to surrender. He's likely to want to fight to the death.'

And so the glorious adventure ended. They had lost.

Then there was the waiting. There was some half-hearted singing, but it soon faded away. No-one had any idea what would happen next. England was in the middle of a war with Germany and any man who deserted the army was being shot.

What would they do to a bunch of Irish rebels who had tried to bring in arms from Germany and had shot at British soldiers?

The order came for the troops to march out from Moore Street. On O'Connell Street, at Nelson's Pillar, they dropped their arms. Michael looked back at the GPO. The flag was still flying. He remembered how Pearse had allowed the youngest Volunteer to raise it. Pearse and the other leaders had been led away – Connolly carried on a stretcher – while most of the GPO garrison were marched to the top of O'Connell Street and into the gardens of the Rotunda hospital. At the Rotunda, they were crowded together on the grass outside the hospital, with hardly room to move – they even had to go to the toilet where they sat or lay. Captain Lee-Wilson, the officer in charge, decided to have some fun at the expense of the rebels. Michael was jerked out of his misery by the sight of Lee-Wilson poking at Tom Clarke with his swordstick. Tom was the oldest of the rebels and had been weakened by years in jail. He had spent fifteen years of his life there, suffering from beatings and starvation. 'Up, me boyo, up there onto the steps. Now take your jacket off. We want to make sure you have nothing hidden away!'

Michael clenched his fists and gritted his teeth. He wanted to take a dive at Lee-Wilson, but what could he do against so many soldiers? This was worse than being roasted alive in the GPO! Tom had a wound on his arm and was slow getting his jacket off. He was not fast enough for Lee-Wilson, who roughly pulled it from his shoulder, making the wound bleed. Clarke looked as if he might faint. He seemed so old and frail. Clarke had kept Michael on track while he was waiting for news of the Rising. 'A bit of patience,' he had said, when Michael had come in cursing one day. 'Use the time to reflect and to plan. Planning is the secret to success!'

Time to reflect. He certainly had plenty of time to reflect now, lying on the cold, wet grass. Some of the passers-by shouted insults at them as they passed the railings. There were a lot of people in Dublin who were angry with the rebels. Some were people who had husbands and sons and brothers fighting in the War. They were earning money that kept families fed, families that would probably go hungry otherwise. They felt the rebels were betraying these young men. Others were people who had respectable jobs, and lived in respectable houses. The way Ireland was suited them and they didn't want to see any changes to it. When Michael thought of the ones who didn't want freedom to get in the way of their comfort, he felt his anger rise. Those people were going to see change, whether they liked it or not. His anger was like a small, hot demon inside him. The demon had to be held down. with gritted teeth and clenched fists. as he watched Tom stripped in the icy wind, mocked at by the little tin-pot soldier. *I'll make him pay*, thought Michael. *I will make them all pay.*

In Prison

Cramped together in the hold, with no blankets, and lifebelts for pillows, the prisoners groaned and snored and prayed and cursed. And once again, the ones with the worst voices seemed to be the ones who thought it was a good idea to sing. His arm held across his nose and mouth, Michael tried to block out the sour smell of his companions. He didn't smell too good himself. It brought back those moments in the schoolyard with Denis holding him down, forcing him to breathe in the smell of unwashed clothes. Many of the men had not been able to change their clothes since Easter Monday. Some of them had been seasick. *Lucky I have a strong stomach*, thought Michael, remembering his first trip to London, so long ago. It was horribly stuffy and pitch dark, but at least, although this was a cattle boat, there were no cows sharing their space.

I could have sung to them in Irish with Mam's songs. Michael smiled in spite of himself. He shifted, trying to get comfortable. It didn't work.

It had been a week filled with fear and confusion. The captured men were marched to Richmond Barracks from the Rotunda. Crowds of people shouted insults at them and some threw stones and spat. It had seemed a very long way to Inchicore. While they were there, some of the prisoners had been taken away. These were the prisoners that the British thought were the most dangerous. It was whispered that they were being taken to Kilmainham Jail. What everyone thought, but nobody said, was that they were being taken away to be executed. Michael probably should have been one of them. In the huge hall in the barracks, he had been put in the line of men who were being herded out of the building. As he stood there, something Joe Plunkett had told him came into his head. So he simply walked from out of the line he had been put in, crossing from one side of the big hall to the other. Joe had told him that the best place to hide was in plain sight. Just do something as if you had the right to do it, and most of the time you could get away with it. Joe had been right. It hadn't worked for Joe himself, though; he was one of the men taken to Kilmainham.

The prisoners were not kept very long in Richmond Barracks. Soon they were sent marching to the North Wall for the boat to England. As they tramped down the Quays, Michael saw a familiar head among the crowds. His cousin Nancy, who had moved back to Dublin, had come to see him being taken away. He immediately began to sing 'On the Banks of My Own Lovely Lee', and she pushed her way over towards him, laughing.

'You still can't sing a note, Mick!'

He laughed, too. Nancy asked him what was happening, but he didn't have any answers to give her. He started to tell her about Seán, but she knew already. There were tears in her eyes as they spoke about their friend. Through the long days, Michael had thought a lot about Seán's death. It was one thing to say you didn't mind dying yourself. It was another to lose a friend like Seán.

Nancy pressed a small packet into Michael's hand – some chocolate and a tightly folded newspaper.

'For the journey,' she whispered, before the heaving crowd pulled her away. 'Tell Susan I'll write!' he called after her. 'Whenever I know where I'm going!'

After they landed in England, there was a long, uncomfortable train journey to Stafford Prison. The building was old and cold but the worst part was that they were all put in separate cells, with no chance to talk and share news. Life was tedious. The one bright spot in every day was when the mail was delivered, and parcels from Michael's friends and family arrived. Michael wrote to Hannie, begging her to send him the fattest novels she could find, along with a French grammar so that he could feel as if he were not entirely wasting his time.

Despite the strict rules, Michael got to know some of the men. He had known some of them slightly from his London days. One was Joe O'Reilly. He was from Bantry, and he and

Michael had long talks about west Cork. Joe was a committed nationalist, but Michael soon discovered that many of the men who had been arrested had little or no connection with the Rising, or with the IRB, the Volunteers or the Irish Citizen Army. Some seemed to have just been picked off the streets. No matter how they had come to be in jail, Michael chatted to them all, and shared the treats that his friends and family faithfully sent to him.

More than chocolate or magazines, what most of the men desperately wanted was news. And slowly, the news seeped through. There had been a string of executions in early May. Whispers came through the walls that Pearse, Connolly, Mac Diarmada and Plunkett had been executed. Connolly had been so ill that he had not been able to stand up, so he was shot in a chair. Sixteen men altogether had been shot. Two other prisoners, Constance Markievicz and Éamon de Valera, escaped death by a hair's breadth. As the executions continued and more young men and boys were imprisoned without trial, people in Ireland started to feel very differently about the rebels.

* * *

'Welcome to Frongoch, Mick.' Joe grinned as he held out his hand. Michael, delighted to see his friend, wrestled him to the ground, and the two of them rolled in the mud until a warder came along and roared at them to get up. Michael had been moved from Stafford to an internment camp in a small valley in the Welsh mountains. Joe had been moved there earlier in the summer. As the two men got up, laughing and brushing the dirt from their clothes, Joe continued:

'I see you haven't changed a bit. It's going to be like old times ... this place is called Frongoch but we call it Francach. If you remember your Irish, that's the word for rat. And the place is full of them. One fellow got bitten under the eye, and got an awful infection, so make sure to check your bed before you go under the blankets – they get everywhere! That old building over there was a distillery, and there are wooden huts up the hill. That's where they'll probably put you. It's hard to say which is worse – the old building is damp but the huts are freezing. Let's just hope we're out of here before the winter comes!'

Michael looked around. 'At least we have the hills and the sky around us – and is that a football pitch over there?'

'Yeah, a Gaelic football one, of course. We have organised athletics and hurling as well. The warders here aren't the worst, apart from one or two bullies. They let us organise debates and classes – you'll have lots of time to work on your Irish.'

Michael breathed in the fresh air. 'It reminds me a bit of home.'

'Well, I hope your home wasn't as full of rats and gnats and flies as this place. And the food is dreadful here, too; you should see the state of the potatoes! I haven't seen a decent piece of meat since we left home. I think the worst days are the ones we get the salt herrings. When they open a barrel, they give us nothing else for dinner for days. And by the time they get to the bottom of the barrel, the fish are stinking.'

Joe wasn't exaggerating about the food; within a few days, Michael was dreaming about the big floury potatoes they had grown at Woodfield.

He was put in one of the huts to start off with, sharing with twenty others. The prisoners there had already set themselves up under a commander. The men in Frongoch considered themselves prisoners of war and expected to be treated as such. They were part of an army, and they were not going to let anyone forget it! The leaders of the 'army' in the camp had already been chosen when Michael arrived. So, although he had plenty of ideas on how things should go, for the first few weeks he had to bite his tongue quite a lot. He was now prisoner 1320, living in Hut 7. He had his own knife, fork, spoon, towel and a bar of soap, a bed made of planks with a straw mattress, and very little else.

There were days that were not too bad. The men organised classes and debates and meetings. Even in the coldest weather, everyone would go out to train or to play sports. Michael, as always, used games and running as a chance to get rid of some of the energy that kept building up inside him, sometimes making him feel as if he might explode. He took part in everything and he still needed to win at any cost. His temper sometimes got the better of him. He hated being stuck at close quarters with people he wouldn't have chosen to spend ten minutes with. Because of this and because he was sometimes a bit pushy, some of his fellow prisoners didn't like him very much. They mocked his Cork accent and his way of twitching his shoulders and tossing his head impatiently when he was annoyed. He heard himself called 'that loudmouth Corkman' and even a bullyboy. After a football match between Cork and Dublin, when Michael had been more than usually rowdy and rambunctious, one of the Dublin Volunteers called over to him:

'Oh, you think you're great! 'Think you're a big fella, do ya?'

* * *

After that comment, Michael, though already bruised and bleeding and exhausted, had to take on the Volunteer as well, just to prove that he was indeed a big fella.

But there were others who admired Michael. They admired how he was able to organise the secret post office in the camp. This involved making friends with the wardens so that things that the prisoners were not allowed to have could be smuggled in and other things could be smuggled out. It meant that news could get past the censor who examined all the letters and parcels. Once again, Michael was haunted by the post office!

Everyone was very excited by the news that many of the people at home in Ireland, shocked by all the executions and the arrests, were now on the side of the rebels.

'Even if it drives me crazy, being here in Frongoch is us doing our bit for the cause ... it's as good publicity as we could possibly get.'

Michael was lying on his bunk, watching his breath curl in the air as he said this. Winter had come and the camp was freezing. All through November, the rain grew heavier, the mud grew muddier, and the rats grew cheekier by the day. On this particular day, the temperature in the camp was below freezing. But snow had fallen overnight. The sky was blue now, and the mountains surrounding the camp were white and beautiful.

Joe, stretched on his own bunk, nodded. Michael continued:

'They're going to have to let us out at some stage, but for the moment we need to be thinking about what to do when that happens. There's no point going for outright rebellion again. We saw that that isn't going to work. We will never be able to defeat the British army in open battle. We have to find other ways. But if we have the ordinary people on our side and ready to help us, we can fight a new kind of battle. A new kind of resistance. The important thing is to have our men and our women organised, knowing what it is they have to do but not knowing too much, in case they're captured.

Look at how Dublin is crawling with spies for the officials in Dublin Castle. We need to have our own network set up. We need to get the ordinary people of Dublin on our side, looking out for us, giving us information. That's the first job to be done.'

Joe raised his eyebrows. 'Are you going to be the one to organise all this, Mick?' he asked.

Michael laughed. 'You never know, I just might be! Now, come on, lads. I heard someone has knocked together a toboggan; let's get out there and give it a go.'

Joe shivered. 'It's too bloody cold out there. I'm staying where I am.'

Michael dived and dragged him from his bunk. One of the other men said, 'You might as well give up the fight, Joe. You know the Big Fella won't.'

Joe groaned and shoved Michael off him. 'Oh, all right, I'll go. Just get off me; you weigh a ton. You must be eating too much!'

'That's the lad!' said Michael. 'And aren't you lucky to have the mittens Hannie knitted for you? I told her that sending some here was the kind of war work she should be doing, instead of knitting them for the British Army. Hurry up!'

Outside, waiting for their turn on the toboggan, Joe started to chat to Gerry Boland. He was the brother of Harry, who Joe and Michael also knew from London.

'Any word from Harry?' Joe asked.

Gerry shook his head. 'Nothing. But have you heard the new rumour? There's talk that we might be let go. After all, they can't keep us here forever. In Ireland, people are furious about so many young men being held without trial. Even in Britain some people feel the same. And then some of the government don't think that keeping all of us together in one place is such a great idea. It's certainly given us the chance to make plans for the future—'

'You're right there,' said Michael. Then he burst out laughing. 'Look at that – the toboggan has gone over. I'm not surprised; it was well overloaded. It's a wonder the warders didn't stop them.'

Gerry made a face. 'Did you not hear what the governor said? He was joking with one of the guards and said that if a few of the lads were killed, there would be fewer mouths to feed.'

Although nobody suffered more than a few bruises from the toboggan rides, soon there *were* fewer mouths to feed in Frongoch. Joe was sent home and Michael really missed him. But as Christmas time grew nearer, his hope that he would be out of the camp himself for the holidays faded.

The men who were left behind in the camp decided to make the best of things. If they were going to be there for Christmas, they might as well organise concerts and plays.

So, it was a shock when half the cast of the forthcoming Christmas show were told they were going home, and even more of a shock when all the remaining men were released on 23 December.

Michael was one of the last to be let go. He left Frongoch in high spirits and made the long, slow journey back to Woodfield. He had to walk the last four miles from Clonakilty to the farm in pouring rain and darkness on the evening of Christmas Day. His suit was shabby and his coat was worn and he felt battered and dirty and exhausted. He didn't care; ahead of him were the lights of home.

He knocked on the farmhouse door, setting the dogs barking. One of Johnnie's children came to answer the knock. When he opened the door, he called out, sounding anxious: 'Dadda, there's a strange man here! But the dogs know him!'

The dogs certainly did know him, and were prancing around him in delight.

Johnnie came from the back of the house, grumbling. 'Who in the name of God is landing on us on Christmas evening in this weather?'

His mouth dropped open when he saw Michael.

Michael grinned widely at the look of shock on his brother's face.

'Ah, it's me all right. Will you let me in? It's perishing out here.'

Johnnie gave him a bear hug, calling to Kathy, 'Come and see what the cat has dragged in!'

Then he held Michael away from him and shook his head.

'Michael, you're going to have to get rid of that stupid little moustache. It will frighten the children and it makes you look like an awful eejit!'

Dublin, 1917

Kathleen Clarke looked even more tired than she had the last time Michael had seen her. That had been before the Rising. Kathleen had lost a husband, a brother and an unborn baby. But her gaze was still as shrewd as it had ever been, as she questioned Michael about Frongoch and then about what he would do if he got the job on offer. The job was organising the Irish National Aid and Volunteers' Dependents' Fund. This fund contained money that was being used to help the families of the many Irish Volunteers who were in jail. With no-one to earn money, many of the families were in a very bad way. Before he went out to fight in the Rising, Tom Clarke had told his wife about money set aside to help these families. Because of the number of people put in prison, many with no trial, more money would have to be raised. Branches of the Fund had been set up all over the country. Now, a secretary was needed to organise raising the money and to decide how it was going to be spent. Michael had applied for the job, and here he was in front of the interview board, sitting on the desk and swinging his legs. Kathleen looked at the rest of the interviewers. Some of them were smiling at this slightly cheeky young man, but some others thought he was a little too confident that he would get the job.

Kathleen had already made up her mind. She knew, and Michael knew, that the money that was being collected could be used for other things as well as helping the families of the men and women in prison. She also knew that it was a perfect position for someone who shared her ideas. She knew that Michael was not only a good organiser, but that he felt the same way she did. The fight to gain freedom had not ended in 1916 – it had just begun.

'You have the job,' she said, giving one of her rare smiles.

Michael couldn't keep the spring out of his step as he made his way down O'Connell Street. Dublin didn't look much better now than it had done just after the Rising. There were gaps everywhere where there had once been shops and cafés and hotels. There were still dozens of burnt-out buildings. Some still had businesses going on the ground floor, but when you looked up, you could see gaping windows and blackened, crumbling stone above. Other features of Dublin hadn't changed for decades, maybe centuries. The doorways were still filled with barefoot children and ragged, skeletal figures, huddled in out of the cold.

Michael's head was buzzing with so many ideas that he hardly noticed the people around him. Not only had he a job – a job he could do well – but this position meant that he was now in the thick of the action. He would be close to the leaders of the Volunteers. He was still in the IRB, and he was getting closer to Sinn Féin. Sinn Féin, led by Arthur Griffith, was the political face of Irish nationalism. Now Michael was part of it all, from the official, political side of the fight for freedom to the secret plotting of the IRB. He was so caught up in his plans that he didn't notice someone coming up behind him until that someone caught at his sleeve. He swung around.

'It's only me, Michael. I surrender!' Nancy held up her hands in mock alarm and laughed.

'Don't go sneaking up on me like that, Nancy. You nearly ended up getting a wallop!'

'You were in a dream, Michael Collins. You could have had a G-man following you and you wouldn't have had a clue!'

Michael laughed too. 'Sure all those bowsies of policemen are too busy watching Mrs Clarke's shop, like they've been doing for years. And much good may it do them. But how are you, Nancy? I haven't seen you for ages! Hold a minute. It's freezing out here. Let's go inside here for a chat. I'll buy you a cocoa – I'm celebrating! And I have a lot of plans I want to talk to you about. Some of them might even involve you!'

Inside the café, Nancy sighed with pleasure and admired the large piece of chocolate cake in front of her. Treats were few and far between these days. But Michael was always generous.

She laughed when she saw the last few crumbs of his cake disappearing into his mouth.

'Well, that was fast! You have a bit of chocolate on your chin, by the way. I see you still have your sweet tooth. I remember your aunt giving out about you when you lived in Inchicore. She said she couldn't keep a cake more than a day or you would have it eaten!'

'It was as well I got out of there. She really didn't want me; she was always giving out about me messing the cushions up in her parlour. I felt too big for the rooms in that house, as if I had only to breathe to knock something over!'

'Well, you did mess her cushions up, because you spent your time throwing them at people. But tell me, why are you looking so delighted with yourself? What are we celebrating?'

'I just got a job as the' – he took a breath – 'Secretary of the Irish National Aid and Volunteers' Dependents' Fund. I'm not sure some of the interviewers were that impressed with me, but they knew that I was the best candidate. I know how to do that kind of work. I'm a good organiser and Kathleen Clarke was on my side. She feels the same way as I do about carrying on the struggle. This is our chance to make the break!'

Nancy nodded. 'Congratulations! It really does seem that things are changing, doesn't it? You can nearly feel it in the air! There's more support for a republic than there has ever been. It's strange to see how things have changed. First there were the executions, then the internments. People have had enough and they're tired of the English promises that never happen. Not to mention being so sick of the war. It seems to be going on forever. And no-one wants Irish lads to be forced into the army!'

'That's the thing though, Nancy. There will have to be more fighting if we're to get our freedom.'

'Can we not do it peacefully, Michael? Surely people will look at our country and realise that we have as much right to be free as a little country like Belgium? Wasn't this war started for the rights of small nations?'

Michael caught the eye of the waitress, who had spent a lot of time hovering near their table. He gave her his best smile and ordered more cocoa. Then he said quietly, 'Was she a bit too interested in what we were saying, do you think?'

'I think she was interested in having a good look at you! But go on, do you think there will be fighting again?'

'There will be. You can be sure that Britain is not going to let Ireland go without a fight. They don't want an example set to places like India and the countries in Africa that are part of their Empire. But we're not going to rush into anything. We don't want another huge mess like the Rising. Don't look at me like that, Nancy. I know they were heroes but it was a mess!'

'I said nothing,' said Nancy. 'But what would you do differently?'

'No big pitched battles – we haven't a chance. It'll be slow; we'll have to smuggle in arms, and train people to use them. And we'll have to work on finding out what's going on at the centre of it all, in Dublin Castle. That's at the heart of the spy rings. My plan is to set up a network of our own men and women to spy on the spies! And I have one picked out already!'

The waitress arrived back with their order. When she had left, Nancy asked: 'And who would that be?'

'That would be you, Nancy, my dear cousin!'

Nancy raised her eyebrows. 'I didn't hear myself offering yet!'

'You've got your transfer to the Post Office here. You'll be in the perfect place to see what's going on and copy documents and telegrams there. I can't believe they don't realise that you're such a close friend, not to mention a cousin! Come on, Nancy; you can do great things for Ireland this way!'

Nancy laughed again, but then became serious.

'And what happens if I do get names for you? What happens to the people we find out are spies?'

'What do you think will happen, Nancy? We'll tell them to get themselves the hell out of Ireland or leave their jobs.'

'And if they don't?'

Michael lowered his voice even further. 'If they don't, they are going to have to be shot.'

There was silence for a moment. Nancy glanced around the teashop to see if anyone was listening. Their waitress was taking an order at a table on the other side of the room and Nancy wondered if she really had been listening in on their conversation, as Michael suspected. This was the kind of talk that could get both of them arrested.

'It's war, Nancy,' said Michael. 'And I promise you that we will be very careful – there are going to be no ordinary people shot, just soldiers and spies. Before we shoot, they will be warned to stop what they are doing. We will have to be sure that we are getting the right people.'

'You have it all figured out, haven't you?'

Michael gave his one-shouldered shrug. 'I've had a lot of time to think and plan over the last few months. I know what we'll have to do to break free. It won't be pretty. But look at the way things are here now. Look around you. Look at the poverty here in Dublin. Look at the way our young men are being slaughtered in a war for the British Empire. Nothing will change as long as we are tied to Britain.'

Nancy nodded. She saw it as a war too.

'So, you collect the money and set up your army of soldiers and spies. But you will still have another problem. How are you going to get the guns and ammunition to fight? You can hardly put an ad in *The Irish Times* – guns required by freedom fighters, apply Box 33!'

Michael laughed.

'I have a couple of ideas. For one thing, we will set up small groups to raid the army barracks and the convoys carrying guns here in Ireland. And I still have contacts in London who can help, who can send us on arms. I will have to set up a smuggling network as well. And we'll need more money than we can raise just in Ireland. We'll have to send someone to raise money abroad. Probably in America, where there are so many Irish people. Whoever goes over will collect money for us and at the same time get the word out about what's happening here. The way people all over the world see us and what we are doing is very important. We will never be able to defeat the British army on a battlefield, but if the opinion of the world is on our side, and we break down all their power here, we just might be able to get the government to cut us loose.'

Nancy finished her drink and stood up.

'So, everything and everyone has to work together. We will be hunting down spies, and fighting the army and police, and battling to get the opinion of the world on our side. And are you going to be at the head of all this, Michael?'

Michael shook his head. 'No, I won't be the overall leader – that will be someone better known, like Dev. After all, he was a commander in the Rising.'

'Dev!' said Nancy, 'I never thought he was your favourite person!'

'Well, I know I'm not his favourite person either. He thinks I'm a west Cork savage. But Nancy, Dev is not the worst when you get to know him, even if he sometimes goes on like old Master Leary. He's a very clever man and he can make wonderful speeches and he has huge support. Anyway, I'll have enough to do, looking after the funds and setting up the network of contacts.'

'But Dev is still in prison. Along with a lot of others, like Harry. What can they do when they're still inside?'

'We'll keep the show on the road until they're let out. We'll be putting Sinn Féin members up for election when places come up in by-elections. Especially if they're in jail. We even have a slogan – 'Put them in to get them out!' The British can hardly leave their MPs in jail, can they? You heard about Joe Plunkett's father getting elected for Sinn Féin in Roscommon? See, it's started already.'

'I saw that. So you're planning more electioneering?'

'Well, the next by-election is in Longford, so the plan is to put Joe McGuinness up for election there. He's still in jail in Lewes. I'll head up to Longford in a few weeks' time to start campaigning. Someone has to do it for him!'

'Hmm,' said Nancy thoughtfully. 'I believe you and Susan are no longer an item.'

Michael pursed his lips and said shortly, 'What has that to do with anything?'

'Ah, come on, Michael, I'm just asking.'

'We're still friends. We will always be friends. But no, we're not as close as we used to be.'

'Don't be getting annoyed ... It's just when you mentioned going to Longford, something came into my head.'

Michael looked at her and said nothing.

Nancy grinned. 'There's a hotel up there in Granard that's very sympathetic to our ideas. It's run by a family of girls and their brother. They're supposed to be charmers so you'd enjoy your stay! It's called the Greville Arms.'

Michael grinned too. 'I might just check it out.'

They left the shop, bundling on hats and scarves in the freezing wind.

'Let's get moving out of this cold. But first, come on over with me to Noblett's and I'll get you some marshmallows and bull's-eyes to celebrate our new jobs. I remember they were your favourites!'

'Trying to bribe me or what! All right, you know it works every time. After that, I have to head back home – I have an early start for work. Where are you heading?'

'I have to see a man about a dog.'

Nancy raised her eyebrows and Michael laughed.

'I'm telling the truth. You know the way I've always loved Kerry Blues? I'm thinking of getting a puppy.'

'Ah, that's great! A dog will be good for you! Some living

creature you can tell your secrets to without worrying they'll be repeated. It will certainly have an exciting life – plenty of travelling, anyway. When are you heading to Longford?'

'Soon. I have a few things to sort out here first.'

'There you go, you're already starting to keep secrets. I hope all this cloak-and-dagger stuff doesn't change you too much.'

Michael swept her into a bear hug.

'Ah, I will always be your favourite cousin. But we might not be able to see each other as much as we used to. I'm going to be very, very busy.'

'It looks like I am, too,' said Nancy. 'I still have to figure out when I will get the time to copy out all those documents for you.'

Granard

The clip-clop of hooves and the faint song of a black-bird were the only sounds as the horses made their way through the winding lanes. Buttercups and cowslips lined the ditches. The roadside hedges were covered in white blossom. The lane was so narrow that sometimes the riders knocked against the blossom and thorns, especially when they tried to ride side by side. Kitty had already torn her blouse and got a nasty scratch from the branches, but she had laughed it off. She seemed to be able to laugh at everything. Michael liked that about her. He liked the whole family. There were five girls and one boy in the Kiernan family; their parents and two of their sisters had died when the children were young. The family was very close and as soon as the children had grown up, they had taken over running the family businesses. Michael breathed in the smell of hawthorn from the hedges. This was a long, long way from Kensington. It was also a long, long way from the filth and boredom of Frongoch, or the noise and squalor and poverty of Dublin. For the first time in ages, Michael felt as if he were at home.

He pulled the reins tighter as Daisy danced a little. The

white horse he was riding reminded him of Gypsy; Daisy, like Gypsy, was a bit of a handful. He wasn't an expert rider by any means, but he could keep his seat on a horse. After all, most of the rides he had taken on Gypsy had been without the help of a saddle or a bridle! He looked around him, thinking that this slow pace was the best way to see the countryside. And in good company too; his companions were the three Kiernan sisters, another young man and Michael's cousin, Gearóid.

Nancy had been right about the Greville Arms in Granard. It was fun staying there. He played tennis and went for picnics and took boating trips on the small lakes nearby. Michael still hadn't confessed to anyone that he didn't know how to swim, just kept his fingers crossed that the boat wouldn't capsize. In the evenings, they played cards or gathered around the piano in the hotel bar. The hotel was a great place to collect local information and meet people who would be likely to support the Sinn Féin candidate in the election. Everyone knew the Kiernan family and the Kiernan family knew everyone. Half the businesses in the town were owned by the family.

Michael and Gearóid had worked hard canvassing for Joe, and they had been successful. Joe had been elected, despite the fact that he was still in prison and had not been able to do any canvassing himself. Now it was time to head back to Dublin. Michael was really going to miss the long chats with the Kiernan family, especially Helen and Kitty. All the girls were charming and funny, and, along with their brother Larry, were enthusiastic nationalists. They were all independent and determined. And such fun!

Michael loved the ease of life in Granard; the comfort of blazing fires and good food, the laughter of the girls and the feeling of being young and healthy and carefree. He watched Helen riding ahead with her friend Paul. Kitty's horse came trotting up beside him. Under her straw hat, Kitty's eyes were full of mischief, 'That pair will make a match of it yet,' she said to Michael.

'Do you think so?' asked Michael. He frowned a little. Helen was very charming and very beautiful.

'And what do you think of Maud and Gearóid?' Michael continued. 'Will they make a match too?'

'Not so fast! Thomas Ashe has been up paying a lot of attention to our Maud! And she's quite keen on him too, I think.'

Michael smiled. 'Well, may the best man win!'

'Oh, we're all great catches!' Kitty laughed and urged her horse ahead.

'We had better head home and see what badness that puppy has got up to while we were out!' she called back over her shoulder.

Convict 242 was called after Michael's friend Austin Stack, who was at present in jail in England. The puppy was too small and too wild to go out with the horses. He thought it was great fun to get under their hooves and try to nip their ankles. A dog of character, he had been shut into Michael's bedroom, where he had managed to make his hurt feelings heard by everyone in the hotel. Michael had carefully locked away his papers and boots, but he hoped he would still have a pillow when he got back.

'He's a devil, isn't he?'

'He is,' said Kitty. 'He will either have to learn to behave with the horses or put up with being left behind. Will you come riding with us tomorrow, Michael?'

Michael shook his head. 'I'm sorry, I can't. I have a pile of things to do before I head back to Dublin on Saturday. But I hope to come down soon again. Will you let me in, even with my demon dog?'

'Of course we will!' said Kitty. 'We'll be happy to see you back! Won't we, Helen?'

Helen turned back towards them and said nothing, just smiled and nodded.

* * *

Back in Dublin, Michael's life was hectic. He was looking after the money for the Volunteers' Dependents' Fund, but at the same time he was busy with other, more secret plans. He had begun to weave his web of contacts. This included everyone and anyone who might be useful to the cause. Some of these were people who worked in Dublin Castle or the Post

Office, like Nancy. Others worked on the railways. Some were ordinary bakers and builders and barmen. All of these people wanted to free Ireland from British rule and were willing to risk their own freedom to help Michael and his comrades. Even the police force had some members who were willing to pass on information. They were in the most dangerous situation of all; if they were found out, they would be considered traitors to the Crown.

There were very few people who knew what Michael was doing, and just two whom Michael felt he could trust with all his secrets. One of these was Joe O'Reilly, who was back in Dublin and had become a kind of secretary to Michael. The other person who knew nearly everything was Harry Boland.

Michael had met up with Harry as soon as his friend had been released from prison. Harry was a lively, slight young man, who was always laughing and almost as full of pranks as Michael himself. He was a tailor and he did his best to keep himself clean and neat, and Michael loved to tease him by wrestling him to the ground when they met. But as well as the horseplay, they spent hours talking about ways and means of getting the information across Michael's new network. Harry had lots of suggestions, including using his tailor's shop in Abbey Street as a front.

'That'll work,' said Michael 'And we can use the dairy in Parnell Square. And Susan has a job in a bookshop in Dawson Street, and she says they'll help us out. Books are a very handy way of passing the messages on – the librarian in Capel Street is one of us, too. What could be more innocent than drinking milk and reading books? And Lily Mernin, one of Béaslaí's cousins, she works in the Castle as a typist and takes a wander with some of my lads in the evenings, pointing out who's who in the army and the police'

'And how is Nancy getting on in the Post Office?'

'The last time I saw her she spent her time giving out that she never has time to eat her lunch, because she spends her lunch-times copying telegrams in the toilets. I tell her it's good for her figure! And she's annoyed that she can't get her hair shingled either, because she needs her bun to hide the papers in!'

He grimaced.

'I had to buy her a stock of bull's-eyes the other day, though – I'm afraid I bawled her out because she sent on a message too late. She didn't realise how important it was. She lost her temper with me and told me I could do my own spying!'

'So you bought her bull's-eyes?'

'Yes, and serenaded her that evening at her digs until she came out to take my peace offering. I explained it was the strain that brought on the bad temper. She told me that I had always had a rotten temper and to go away and stop annoying her! She was afraid the neighbours would give out! It was after midnight.'

'I'm sure they did give out; you still can't sing a note. Though I hear you've been serenading some young ladies in Granard!'

Michael tossed his head impatiently.

'Ah, those Kiernans are great girls – they have had a sad past, but they go along as if they haven't a care in the world! You will have to come up and meet them sometime, Harry.'

'Well, I'd love to, but it can't happen just yet. We need to be working hard on the East Clare election. Do you think Dev will get in?'

'I will make bloody sure he does!'

'Is he still mad with you for going ahead with putting Joe McGuinness up for election in Longford?'

Michael shrugged. 'He's happy enough now we have a prisoner elected!' he said impatiently. 'Ah, Harry, you know Dev; it's my way or the highway with him. He'll get over it when he gets himself elected in East Clare!'

'What do you really think of Dev, Mick?' Harry was curious. He had huge admiration for Éamon de Valera. De Valera's way of behaving was quieter, and, thought Harry ruefully, much more dignified than Michael's. There was no way he would wrestle you to the ground just to say hello. But he was not sure that Michael felt the same way as he did about the man who, with Arthur Griffith of Sinn Féin, was the acknowledged leader of the movement.

'I respect him. I think he's the one to lead us. He's more of a politician than I'll ever be; that's for sure. He can make speeches. And he is totally sincere.'

'But?'

'But sometimes he drives me mad, the way he speaks to me like a schoolmaster. And I lose my patience when he takes forever to make up his mind.'

'Has he been giving you a hard time about being in the IRB?'

'You too? He says it goes against his conscience, the idea of a secret society. We need secrets these days, Harry. It's the only way we are going to get where we want to be.'

Weaving the Web

It was a bright spring morning in 1918 and the streets of Granard were lined with cheering crowds. They were cheering for Michael. Kitty, Helen and Maud were at the door of the Greville Arms, ready to welcome him. Michael had just been released from Sligo Jail. He had been arrested for making speeches against the government. Although he had hated his time in jail, he would have stayed there if he had not been told to go out on bail. His work was too valuable to leave him locked away.

'Was it awful, the jail?' Kitty asked. 'Helen said that when she went to see you, the conditions were dreadful.' They were sitting around the range in the kitchen of the hotel. Kitty, for once, looked and sounded serious.

'Ah, sure I'm here now with you and I can forget about it. It was great to see Helen, and my sister Katie came to visit me too. But the days were very long. The thing that really drove me crazy was not being able to do anything, when I know how much there is to be done. Everyone else is out there taking huge risks!

'What sort of risks?' asked Kitty.

Michael thought for a moment.

'Well, there's one girl – she's one of our information gath-erers in Dublin. She hides in one of the big wicker baskets of mail that are shipped over to England, going through the letters. Looking for anything that might be of use to us or is of too much use to the other side. She does the trip over to Liverpool and back again, hiding in the basket. If she was caught, she'd be put in jail for a very long time.'

'Ah, tell us her name, or at least what she looks like!' said Kitty.

Michael shook his head. He thought of tiny Dilly, valiant and smiling, who played the piano for the silent movies. He couldn't risk mentioning her name to anyone! He had become an expert at keeping secrets. The less each person knew about what his or her colleagues were doing, or even who they were, the better chance everyone had of surviving. This meant that a great deal depended on Michael keeping things in his head, as notes and diaries were a risk to everyone, too. He did keep one small notebook with him, though. Years working as a clerk and as an accountant had made him very organised. He smiled sometimes to think that he had learned all these skills while working at the heart of the British Empire, in London.

'I can't give out any names, you know that. I couldn't live with myself if she were caught. If she went to jail, she would probably go on hunger strike with the other women and who knows what might happen then?'

Everyone thought of Thomas Ashe, Maud's fiancé. He had been arrested in August and, like many others, he went on hunger strike. The prisoners were protesting against being treated as common criminals, not as political prisoners. He had died as a result of food being forced into his stomach.

'It's a crazy world we live in,' Helen said. 'But I think you enjoy the danger and the craziness, Mick!'

He laughed. 'I'd be lying if I said I didn't, a little. I couldn't wait to get out of jail and back into the thick of things. This is our golden moment, our chance to make the dreams of the past become real.'

He laughed again, a little embarrassed. 'Does that sound very pompous?'

The girls laughed too. Then Kitty said: 'Well, no-one can accuse you of not having big ideas! But what's the next step?'

'We will wait until the war is finished. It might really be over by this Christmas! When it's over, there will have to be a general election. Then, if Sinn Féin gets into government with a majority, we'll have the right to go out and fight for freedom. The Irish people will have given us that right, because they will have voted to be free of the British Empire. We'll be the army of the elected representatives of Ireland!'

'And if there is no majority?' Kitty was leaning forward in excitement.

'There will be. The feeling is out there. The only part of Ireland that won't vote for Sinn Féin will be the northeast and Belfast.'

'But what if Sinn Féin won't agree with a war, with violence? Arthur Griffith has never agreed with violent methods.'

'Griffith is the leader of Sinn Féin, but most of the members are ready and willing to fight. Sinn Féin today is very different from the days before the Rising. And we have a kind of pact now, between the Volunteers and Sinn Féin and the IRA. We all want the same thing in the end. All through the centuries, fighting and squabbling amongst ourselves has been one of the reasons why we never got anywhere! So it's time now for us all to work together.'

'But will it not bother you,' Helen said, 'shooting people or giving the orders to have them shot?'

'I saw people killed in the Rising, Helen. I know it's a terrible thing to take a life. But if it's a war, it's a war. Look at how many people have been killed during the past few years in France and in Belgium – so many soldiers from all over the world. Millions of young men. America went into that war because it was supposed to be about fighting against the might of the German empire, because it was trampling on the rights of small nations. Well, we are a small nation and we have the right to fight for our freedom. In a war, people get killed. The British will never let us go unless we put up a fight. And unless we get rid of the spies and the RIC men and the soldiers. And the informers on our own side.'

'Ah, girls,' he continued, seeing the expression on their faces. 'Don't think I take this lightly. I know what the pain of losing someone you love is like, and all the men who will be killed have wives or children or parents who love them. If I saw any other way of doing this, I swear to you, I'd do it. I'll just have to make sure that we get the right people!'

Escape!

I t was a dark February evening, and Michael and Harry were driving along a small road close to Lincoln Jail. They left the car and started to make their way across the drenched, muddy fields that surrounded the prison walls.

'Time for the signal, Harry!' whispered Michael. Their timing needed to be exactly right. This escape plan had involved a lot of planning and even more cake. Harry took out his pocket torch and flashed it a number of times towards the wall of the jail.

'That's enough, Harry, said Michael. You don't want the guards down on top of us!' Harry was fumbling with the torch, which was still flashing brightly. His face had become very red. 'Harry, hurry up!'

'I can't get the bloody thing off!'

This was a disaster. If they went any closer to the jail walls, the torch would be a beacon, saying: 'Look at us! We are coming to free some of your prisoners!'

Michael couldn't help a small snort of laughter. 'Better get a better brand the next time we do something like this!' he said. He grabbed the torch from Harry and tried to switch it off himself. It kept flashing brightly.

There was a curse or two and, in the end, Harry had to hide the torch deep in the pockets of the large fur coat he was wearing. They had to keep going. It was vital to get Dev back to Dublin.

Some months before, there had been a round-up of important Republican figures. They had been accused of collaborating with the Germans, but no evidence had been produced for the charges. This was because the charges were completely made up, so there was no evidence to produce.

Michael had escaped capture but De Valera had not, and he had been re-elected as an MP while still in prison. Soon after Dev arrived in Lincoln Prison, he noticed that there was a door in the exercise yard, which led through the high wall that surrounded the jail. He had got hold of the prison chaplain's keys and had made a drawing of the key for that particular door. He had then managed to get a picture of the key to Michael, first disguised in a comic Christmas card and then hidden in a drawing. As a result, two keys had been smuggled in to De Valera, baked into cakes and delivered to the prison. But one key was too small and the other not quite the right shape. Michael had been furious when the news came that the second key had failed. He muttered that his codename for this operation, which was Field, should be changed to Goldilocks. Nothing was ever quite right!

In the end, yet another cake was sent in with a blank key, and De Valera managed to get a friend in the prison to file it to the right shape. Michael and Harry had brought a fourth key with them, as a backup. And now it was time to see if their plan would work. The prisoners were to make their way to the door in the exercise yard. A man singing in Irish outside the walls had told them the time to start watching for the signal. Dev and his two fellow prisoners, Seán McGarry and Seán Milroy, were waiting at the door when they heard a shuffle outside.

'Are you there, Dev?'

Michael's voice was a harsh whisper.

'*Táimid anseo*,' said Dev, never one to miss an opportunity to speak Irish.

Michael pushed in the new key they had brought with them, hoping that it would work. He jiggled it and turned it sharply, then let out a string of curses.

'What is it?' De Valera's polite tone held a note of reproach as well as alarm. He didn't approve of Michael's colourful language.

'Hell and damn and blast, I'm after breaking the cursed key in the lock. I'm sorry, Dev. I just thought if I pushed it a bit harder, it would work!'

'Brute force and ignorance does not always win the day,' said Dev. They could hear him sniff and mutter something

104

else on the other side of the door. Michael met Harry's eye and, despite themselves, they grinned. Dev never cursed, but that had sounded very like one! There was a short prayer in Irish and something else rattled in the lock, this time from the other side of the door. The broken key clattered to the ground at Michael's feet. De Valera had used the key made in the jail to push the broken key out of the lock. Then there was the sound of a key turning. The door opened and Dev, McGarry and Milroy came out, all grinning broadly. When De Valera turned to lock the door after him, Michael growled: 'We've no time to be polite and lock up after us. Get those socks off your boots and let's get going! By the way, Harry is your girlfriend if anyone meets us.'

Dev gave the smile that completely transformed his face.

'It's a pity I'm too tall to act the lady – I could do with that fur coat!'

Harry took a somewhat battered lady's hat from his pocket and gave a twirl as he pulled it over his hair.

'Amn't I the belle of the breakout?'

'Quit fooling. We have to move.'

They passed off-duty soldiers chatting with some girls and exchanged a friendly goodnight with them. The girls had been recruited by Michael to keep the soldiers busy. Back at the car, everyone breathed a sigh of relief. The plot had worked. Éamon de Valera, President of Dáil Éireann, was free.

The Dáil was the new body that had been set up as the government of Ireland. Michael's prediction had been right. Sinn Féin swept the board in 1918, in the elections that were held soon after the war ended in November. They were historic elections, not just because they let the world know that most Irish people wanted to be free of British rule, but because, for the first time ever, women could vote. And in Ireland, the very first woman was elected to the British Parliament. She was Constance Markievicz, who had fought in the 1916 Rising and narrowly avoided execution. But Constance did not take her seat in the Westminster Parliament. Like so many of her Sinn Féin companions, she was in prison when she was elected.

The Sinn Féin deputies who were not in jail met in the Mansion House in Dublin and formed a government. De Valera was elected as the President of the first Dáil in January 1919. Soon after, the first shots of what would later be called the War of Independence were fired, at an ambush of the police in Soloheadbeg, County Tipperary. The Volunteers who planned the ambush in Tipperary were not acting under orders. But the Volunteers, the IRB and most of the Sinn Féin members were agreed that the time had come to act. It was time for the battle to begin. Using force was justified. The people had spoken. The British had no right to rule Ireland. The three strands of the web Michael had been helping to weave had now all come together.

Michael was elected too, and became the Minister of Finance, but he wasn't in the Mansion House on the day the first Dáil met. Neither was Harry Boland, though the records show that they were present. This was a cover, to hide what they were really up to and where they really were. Both men were in England, in the thick of planning the escape of Dev and his two comrades. The success of the breakout was very embarrassing for the British authorities.

A few weeks later, in the back of a modest tailor's shop in Abbey Street in Dublin, Harry put water to boil on a spirit stove and looked at his friend critically.

'I don't know whether you should use this water for a shave or for a cup of tea! You're a desperate-looking villain ... what have you been up to?'

Michael sat down, straddling one of Harry's wooden chairs, rocking it backwards and forwards. He was, thought Harry, in flying form. Which usually meant he had been up to something very dangerous.

Michael had a friend with him on this visit. Harry regarded Convict 242 sternly. Like Michael, Convict 242 tended to be a bit overenthusiastic in his greetings, and Harry didn't want either hair or mud all over his trousers.

'Sit!' he said. The dog looked at him and scratched himself thoughtfully. He did not sit.

'He doesn't pay a blind bit of attention to anyone but me,'

said Michael, stroking 242. 'Or even to me, sometimes. He has a mind of his own, that fella.'

'Well, you shouldn't have given him Austin Stack's prisoner number as a name! You know how stubborn Austin can be!'

'Ah, but Austin is from Kerry too! And the hair is a bit like his. Not to mention the temper.' They both laughed. Austin Stack was a good friend of both of them but he wasn't the easiest man to get along with.

'Mick, for God's sake, be careful with that chair. It's an old one and can't take that kind of treatment!'

Michael ignored him and continued rocking.

Sometimes, thought Harry, he's like a big child. But sometimes that's one of the nicest things about him!

'Oh, sit down,' said Michael, 'so I can tell you about last night. I had a great time. Our good friend Ned has pulled quite the trick!'

'Policeman Ned? Ned Broy?'

'The very one! Well, didn't he manage to get a key to the safe in Brunswick Street police station – where there are large quantities of very interesting files! So we decided to pay a visit. He was on duty there late last night and let us in. I brought along one of the young Volunteers – that'll be a story for him to tell his children! We walked in, as brazen as you like, with all the RIC men snoring their heads off upstairs, and spent the night going through the files. I don't know what we'd do without Ned Broy! Between himself and our friends in the Castle we've got more and better information than we've ever managed! We got a lot of names last night, Harry, a lot of names.'

'It was an awful risk, though, Mick? Any of the RIC men could have woken up and come downstairs.'

'Ah, sure Ned had locked the door. It was more of a risk for him than for us. But wait until I tell you what they said about me, Harry. It seems I am from a brainy west Cork family with Sinn Féin sympathies. I laughed so hard Broy gave out to me. Hannie and Katie and the rest will be delighted to hear that the Collins family has a reputation for brains!'

Harry threw his eyes up to Heaven.

'You have a reputation for being the biggest eejit under the sun and for taking the most risks!'

Michael dived at him.

'Mind the water, Mick – it's boiling. I wish you would remember that I'm a tailor and I can't go around looking like something the cat dragged in. Which I usually do after I've been in your company for a few minutes. And will you please stop that dog getting overexcited?'

'Don't be so grumpy, Harry.'

'I'm not grumpy. I'm only a bit fed up that you didn't bring me along for the fun of it!'

'We couldn't risk you being caught. You're the golden boy

at the moment! You do know that Dev has plans for you, don't you?'

Harry nodded gloomily.

'Yes, he wants me to go to America to set things up for him before he heads over in the summer. He says he needs me to help him to raise money and to let people over there hear the voice of Ireland's people. But I'd rather be here in the thick of things. Apart from anything else, I want to make sure you're not going to take over Kitty Kiernan's affections! I'm sure if I keep at it, I'll get her to go out with me!'

Michael stopped rocking. 'I still don't think that Dev should just take off and leave us here without a leader. We sprang him from Lincoln so he could be here! Griffith could surely go instead.'

'Griffith doesn't have the same power or popularity. We need money, Mick.'

'It's true. We do need more money for arms if we want to keep the battles against the RIC going all over the country. In Cork, they're flying through the ammunition ... But I still think Dev should be here. And you're a huge loss to us here.' He paused and smiled. 'As for Kitty Kiernan? Who knows what will happen there? She'll probably find some respectable solicitor like her sister has and forget about both of us! But I'm sure no matter what happens, Harry, you and I will always be friends.'

'That's all very well, but I still want to be part of the excitement here!' He glanced away for a minute. 'Look at that bloody dog! Still scratching! The pair of you must be passing on fleas to every safe house in the city ... Here. Take your tea. You need it after your busy night.'

Convict 242 stopped scratching. He sat upright and stared intently at Harry. He knew where every stash in Dublin was buried. And he knew that very soon, Harry would crack and give him a dog biscuit from the store hidden in his desk.

Secret City

Harry wasn't missing very much fun at the moment, thought Michael, a few months later, as he looked down from the skylight to where the ladder was supposed to be. There was no ladder. Bloody painters, he supposed. He sighed. He really didn't have any choice. If he ever got his hands on whoever had told the Castle about their new head-quarters, that person would be very sorry, very soon! He'd find out, and he would make sure they would never again have the chance to open their big mouth. He looked down again, remembering the drop through the loft in the Wood-field house when he was tiny. His sisters swore he couldn't possibly remember the accident, but there were nights he dreamed of the fall and woke up shaking, his hand reaching for his revolver.

Far below him, there was a small square landing, and then a very long drop down steep stairs. Nothing for it. It would be only a matter of minutes before the soldiers found the sky-light he had climbed through and came crawling across the roof after him. Slowly, carefully, he let himself down through the skylight and, swinging backwards and forwards, lined up his body as closely as he could to the landing. A few inches the wrong way and he would be hurtling down thirty feet to the bottom of the stairs. He took a breath and let himself drop.

His ribs hit hard against the banisters and he felt one or two of them crack, but his feet were on the landing and there was no time to hang around nursing himself. He made his way down the stairs and out the front door of the hotel, making sure to have a good look at the soldiers parked outside the neighbouring house, his new headquarters. They wouldn't find much in there – his good friend Batt O'Connor was an expert at making hidden cupboards for storing secrets.

Casually, as if he were just another businessman leaving the Standard Hotel, he joined the small crowd that was watching the raid. Would they arrest any of the girls? His secretary Sinéad was led out, but it looked as if only the men were being taken away. Michael breathed a sigh of relief. If the women had been searched, the soldiers would have found the gun he had thrown to one of them before making his exit. He caught Sinéad's eye but she knew better than to let any expression appear on her face. Whistling carelessly, he nodded at the soldiers as he made his way down Harcourt Street. He would have to wait until tomorrow to collect his bicycle.

* * *

Michael, along with most of the members of the Dáil, was on the run. Ireland was in chaos. There were raids all over the country; some of them were by the army and police, others by the Volunteers, who were now the official army of the Dáil. Raids and roadblocks disrupted everyone's daily life. In Dublin especially, watching raids was now the main form of entertainment. Other kinds of entertainment, such as dances and shows, had suffered, because curfew meant that everyone had to be inside from a certain time in the evening until the next morning. But there was also a spirit of quiet resistance among ordinary people. Railwaymen refused to carry British troops or ammunition on their trains, and men in RIC police uniforms were refused service in shops and cafés and bars. Even in the schools, the children of policemen were not spoken to by their classmates and sometimes came home in tears after a day of being ignored. Many police left the force and left Ireland, their memories of home full of bitterness.

Many of those who stayed lost their nerve. They saw enemies at every street corner and behind every bush, and suspected that arms and guns were hidden everywhere. In Dublin, they felt that they were living in a city where nothing was quite what it seemed. In many ways, they were right. There was a secret, invisible city operating in the heart of the capital: a cycle shop in Parnell Square where grenades were made; a carpenter's shop in Abbey Street where the staff was never available for work; a dapper tailor who was always too booked-up to make any suits; a cobbler who was an expert at fitting secret documents into the soles of shoes; smiling young women who walked through roadblocks with messages sewn into their petticoats or packed into babies' nappies.

And guns were everywhere. In the bakeries, there were guns piled into the ovens. There were guns under floorboards, hidden up chimneys, stashed away in specially made secret compartments, in toilet cisterns and hen-houses and pig-pens. Pistols in butter boxes, rifles in egg cases. Gold, too. One of Michael's jobs was to organise collecting money for the new government and he had special hiding places for it. Some of it went into the accounts of respectable members of society, but some of it was turned into gold sovereigns and gold bars, and was buried under the floorboards in a particular house in Donnybrook. The house belonged to Batt O'Connor. Batt, the master carpenter, was kept very busy making secret cupboards and secret rooms in houses all over the city.

Just as important as the guns and the money was information. And here there was a network too, of barmen and clerks, messenger boys and shop assistants. Spies in the Castle, like David Neligan, passed messages about the latest Dublin Castle plans to friendly hotel porters and receptionists. Ned Broy dropped into a certain dairy every morning and had a glass of milk, even though he hated milk. Young men and women popped into

Capel Street Library or O'Hegarty's bookshop, and picked a book they thought no-one would ever want to read, sliding a secret message between the pages. Dilly Dicker continued her journeys back and forth to England by mail boat, and Nancy's supervisor called her into her office, concerned for her health as she was spending so much time in the bathroom. Nancy had been given a promotion. Put in charge of handling the coded messages for Dublin Castle, she was busier than ever. Michael roared with laughter when he heard the news.

At the centre of it all was Michael, organising everything from fundraising to prison escapes. In October, he organised the escape of his friend Austin Stack and some of his companions from Strangeways Prison in England. Other escapes followed, including a mass breakout over the wall of Mountjoy Jail. During that escape, the escapees were even helped by some of the warders!

Michael continued to saunter through this invisible city. He cycled or walked or sometimes took the tram, stopping to look at raids and chatting to soldiers at roadblocks. When he took the tram, he always sat upstairs, near what was called the destination box. This was the box at the front of the tram that held the sign to show where the tram was going to. It was the best place to hide any secret papers, or even a gun, if the tram were stopped by soldiers. This happened to him more than once, but Michael always kept his cool. Hiding in plain sight, he managed to avoid being caught, though his friends wondered when his luck would run out, as it surely must.

Between organising prison breaks, smuggling arms and keeping his new spy network going, along with his job as Minister of Finance, there were not enough hours in the day for Michael. He often spent half the night awake, working while others slept. As he rarely spent more than one night in any house, poor Convict 242 didn't see him very often. Sometimes Michael had stomach aches and sometimes he lost his temper when people didn't do their job properly. Even some of the other government ministers found that he didn't suffer fools gladly. But despite the endless work and the narrow escapes, 1919 ended on a high note for Michael. Things were moving fast. The job of making a new Ireland was well underway. That Christmas, he managed to make a visit home to Woodfield. He also went to the Kiernans for the New Year.

Kitty, thought Michael, really was a terrible flirt. He sat in one of the big armchairs and watched her playing the piano, smiling at him. She sang:

I know where I'm going
I know who's going with me
I know who I love
But the dear knows who I'll marry.

Who would Kitty marry? She had already been engaged to someone but had broken it off. Michael knew that Harry had been totally bowled over by her and wrote her long letters from America. It had made things awkward between the friends, but both of them were determined that it would not ruin their friendship.

Do I know who I love? Michael wondered. *I thought I loved Helen ... but she didn't love me. And now I'm getting fonder and fonder of Kitty ... Do I know where I'm going or who I really am? Who am I? The loud, bossy, twitchy person who loses his temper too often? The eejit who finds entertainment in ruining Harry's outfits and throwing his boots out the window? Or the quieter Michael, dreaming of a new Ireland, an Ireland at peace and finally looking to the future, not the past? But will there be peace? Will we ever get peace while the Unionists in the north want nothing to do with us?*

That was one of the huge problems about Ireland becoming a Republic. The Unionists still didn't want it to happen, and the British government had brought in a new Act, with two separate parliaments planned for the north and the south. They thought that giving the south of Ireland Home Rule was the solution. But most people in Ireland felt that what was being offered was too little, too late.

Michael sighed and tossed his head. It was hard to stop thinking about work, even in this warm and cheerful room, with music and laughter all around him. He missed Harry, and the news he was sending home was worrying. The visit of the Irish seemed to be causing rows in America. Dev was taking every chance of publicity, including dressing up in a Choctaw chief's headdress that made him look ridiculous – he seemed to be taking his nickname of The Chief a bit too seriously! Michael did have some sympathy for Dev. It must be hard for him to be away from his wife and his little children, for so long.

Michael promised himself that he would continue his weekly visits to the De Valera household in Greystones, to share any news he had with Sinéad, and to give her Dev's salary. Sinéad was amazing; she had nursed her children through the flu epidemic, she kept a warm and welcoming home for everyone, and she dealt with almost every family crisis on her own. And Michael loved to spend time with the children. They were full of life and it was an escape from all the worries that kept him awake at night.

Kitty had finished singing. She came over to him. 'I don't think you heard a word of my song! You were miles away there on your own, Michael. Will you not give us a song yourself?'

'Do you want the room cleared or not?' Michael laughed at the old joke and swung her around as he stood up. 'Let's dance instead! Let's dance in the New Year, Kitty! Maybe it will be the first year of the Irish republic! Whatever happens, I'm sure it's going to be a good one! Will you get up early and walk up to the Moat with me, so we can see the sun rise on the New Year? The view over the river and towards the lake is lovely, and the weather is set to be fine!'

'Maybe I will,' said Kitty. 'And maybe I won't!'

Neither of them could know that 1920 was to bring with it some very dark times.

War!

All over Ireland, small squads of men had gone to war. It wasn't a war where huge armies faced each other over battlefields. It was a war of raids on police barracks, of men taken out of their houses to be shot because they were suspected of being informers. There were brutal actions on both sides. It was an ugly war, but no more ugly than the Great War that had killed millions of young men just a few years before. Nevertheless, Michael sometimes wondered what they had started. Sometimes he looked at the young men he was sending out into terrible danger and wondered if the great ideal of Ireland as a nation could be worth all this blood. And despite all his efforts, sometimes the wrong people were killed. Once, a young recruit asked him if it never bothered him that so many people were dying – men women, and sometimes even children. Michael exploded.

'Does it bother me?' he roared. 'Of course it bloody bothers me. But this is war, though the British refuse to call it that. We are fighting for our freedom. We are making the sacrifice so that men and women in the future can have an Ireland that is ruled by themselves, not by a crowd in London who don't give a tinker's curse about us and think we're all savages anyway.'

'Then why don't they just let us go?'

'They won't let us go because they are afraid of the Unionists and they are afraid the rest of their Empire will look at us and try to get the same thing – that's why.'

'What will happen to the north? Do you think the Unionists will ever agree to be part of the Republic?'

'They're our people too. We can't just cut them off and forget about them. What we have to do is make sure that the new Ireland we're making feels like a home to them, that they are not made to feel unwanted or treated badly. That their voices are listened to and their opinions respected. If we don't do that, we'll just be acting the same way the British are acting towards us. And we need the whole country. We need different ways of looking at things, different kinds of people. We have to make sure that Ireland has room for all her people. Now, get on with what you were doing and let me get on with my work. That's the way to make all this end more quickly – get on with it. Get the Hell out of my office and stop wasting my time!'

The Volunteer left very quickly indeed. Nobody hung around when the Big Fella lost his cool.

Michael, sometimes short-tempered, sometimes full of an angry sort of energy, got on with the work at a ferocious pace, though his health suffered from the stress and lack of sleep.

From the beginning of 1920, the British government had clamped down harder and harder on Ireland – not just on the Volunteers but also on ordinary people. In March, a new group of men were sent to help the RIC keep order. The members of the police force had got tired of being targets of the Volunteers and of being boycotted by local people. What had once been a respectable job had become a nightmare, and the numbers of policemen continued to fall. More men were needed to try to keep order in Ireland.

Many of the men who were sent from Britain to support the RIC had fought in the recent war in Europe; they had seen and done terrible things. They were used to fighting in straightforward battles where you went in and killed or were killed. They looked on their job as a simple one: crush any resistance to British rule! They didn't have a proper uniform and were called the Black and Tans because the colours they wore were like the colours of one of the Irish packs of hunting dogs who had that name. And they acted like hunters. They didn't care about the Irish people. They were serving in a country where they felt hated and spied on and in danger at every moment, and many of them had been left shell-shocked as a result of the war. So they soon gained a name for themselves as brutal and ruthless; they carried out revenge shootings of people who had done nothing, just ordinary people going about their business. They were later joined by another force, called the Auxilaries, known as Auxies. These men were similar to and perhaps even more brutal than the Tans in the way they carried out the business of 'keeping the peace'.

The IRA, as the Dáil army was now known, committed many terrible deeds also. Dozens of big country houses were burned down, either because of the landlords' sympathy with British rule or because there was the possibility they might be used as a barracks. Old and young were killed if they were suspected of having given information to the Crown forces. In Cork, one old lady who had given information about a planned ambush was taken out to a barn. She and her chauffeur were shot dead while her house went up in flames. Young girls, suspected of being too friendly with the British military, had their heads shaved as punishment.

In September, everyone in Ireland had been horrified by what had happened in Balbriggan, a small fishing town north of Dublin. The Auxies had set fire to the town in revenge for the death of two of their men, simply because the killing had happened in one of the pubs in the village. Late at night, a convoy of lorries arrived and Auxies went crazy in the streets. Thatch was set on fire and the flames spread along the rows of little cottages, while the raiders ran around, shooting and shouting and attacking totally innocent people. Terrified families ran from the village, hiding in ditches and barns. Many were injured and dozens of people lost their homes and their businesses. Two of the prisoners taken were beaten to death at the Black and Tans' barracks in Quay Street.

The Auxiliaries went on the rampage in Granard too, because an RIC man was shot while at the bar of the Greville Arms hotel. Michael got news that Kitty and her sisters had been arrested. The Kiernan sisters had been held for a few days and questioned about their connections with Michael and Harry. When they were released and returned to the hotel, they found it burnt to the ground, along with many other buildings in Granard.

The British had also been busy arresting anyone suspected of being involved in the fight for independence. In the prisons, Republicans went on hunger strike and were left to die. Terence MacSwiney, the Lord Mayor of Cork, died on hunger strike in Brixton Prison. Many British people, as well as many people from all over the world, looked on in horror at what the British government was doing. The horror continued with the hanging of a young medical student, Kevin Barry, who had been captured when taking part in an ambush. The fact that he was eighteen made the execution seem even more horrible.

In some ways, the clampdown on anyone involved in anti-British activity, with more and more suspects arrested, helped the IRA. For a start, it turned public opinion in Britain and indeed all over the world. The government troops seemed to be out of control and it was very clear that their actions were not supported by the people of Ireland, who kept on voting for Sinn Féin. Men went on the run to avoid arrest and, living away from home and unable to work, they organised themselves into small groups called 'flying columns'. The flying columns attacked British strongholds and then moved on. In the wilder parts of Cork and the southwest, these men knew the land, knew who would shelter them, and could do serious damage. But to do any damage at all, they needed arms and ammunition.

This was one of Michael's big problems; it was getting harder and harder to supply them. He became more and more stressed and short-tempered, mostly with those closest to him, like Joe O'Reilly. Never enough money, never enough arms, never enough time. He became even more impatient with the people he felt were not doing a good job. This meant that some of them resented him.

This was the case with Cathal Brugha, the Minister of Defence, who was jealous of Michael. It was also the case with his old friend Austin Stack. He felt sad about Austin's resentment. They had been good friends in the days after 1916. But things came to a head on the day Michael stood up in front of the Dáil and told Austin that everyone knew his government department was a joke. Even as he said it, he realised from the look on Austin's face that there was no going back: Austin had turned against him. Like many others, he felt that Michael had no respect for him. From that day, Cathal and Austin no longer referred to Michael as the Big Fella, as so many others did. It had become a term of respect and admiration. These days, Cathal and Austin called Michael 'Mickeen'.

There were still some brighter days. Michael celebrated his thirtieth birthday by entering Convict 242 in a dog show. The dog had finally learned to behave himself and won first prize, which was presented by a British army captain. The show was filled with army officers and Dublin Castle officials. Michael delighted in the idea of having been right under the nose of the very people who had offered a reward for his capture. But these good days were becoming rarer and rarer.

And in November 1920, the darkest day of all arrived.

Bloody Sunday

'It's done.'

The first member of the Squad was reporting back to Michael.

'Good work; the air in Dublin is cleaner for it,' he said.

Neither man smiled.

A young recruit, working with Michael in the headquarters, burst out: 'That's brilliant! Let's have a toast to that.' He raised his teacup.

'Put that down,' Michael snarled. 'It needed to be done and it's done and I don't regret it. But we will have no toasts to men being killed, and the sooner you learn that, the better. Wait until you see a man die in front of you. You'll know what a serious thing it is to take someone's life.'

The assassin nodded. He was a tough man, but he felt sick to his stomach. He had shot the man in front of his wife, knowing that his children were asleep in bed upstairs. He had heard one of them wake and call out as the shot was fired.

Michael's Squad members had to be tough. There were twelve of them and their job was a simple one – to kill British intelligence officers. Today was a red letter day. The most famous group of spies – known as the Cairo gang because they sometimes met at Café Cairo on Grafton Street in Dublin – were a huge threat to the new army and to the Dáil. Michael had made a bold plan to have each one of them shot on this Sunday morning, 21 November 1920. Now the news was trickling back. Not all of the assassinations had been a success. Of the thirty-five killings planned, eleven men had been killed and a further one would not survive for long. Some of these men had been on their way from mass; some were just sitting down to their Sunday breakfast. Some were dragged from their beds.

At lunchtime, Michael heard someone thundering up the stairs. Joe came rushing into the office.

'Mick, Mick,' he shouted breathlessly. 'You'll have to do something!'

Michael looked up from the list of figures he was working on. He had been concentrating hard. Sometimes it helped to look at the most mundane, ordinary stuff. It kept his mind off other things. At the moment, he wanted to keep his mind off the fact that three young men had been captured the evening before, and that there was very little he could do to save them. No doubt they would be shot or hanged like young Kevin Barry. He looked down again and frowned at the page in front of him – a request for more arms, from a small battalion in Kerry. Some of the Volunteers seemed to be very bad at counting. How could 200 rounds of ammunition be supplied, 47 be used and the company have only ten left? He scribbled a reply – *Are yiz using the bullets to shoot rabbits or what?* – and signed off.

He turned to Joe. 'Sit down there, Joe,' he said calmly. 'And tell me what's the matter.'

'It's the game in Croke Park, Mick. You know the way you sent word that it should be cancelled, it being the day that was in it?'

Michael nodded grimly. He had told the GAA that going ahead with the football match would risk a bloodbath of reprisals from the Tans and the Auxies.

'The GAA has decided it's too late to cancel,' Joe said. 'There are massive crowds in Croke Park already and they say that getting them to leave might result in people being hurt in the crush. The match is going to go ahead.'

Michael let out a long string of colourful curses.

'Eejits, what the hell do they think they're doing? If that game goes ahead, the Auxies or the Tans are bound to use it as an excuse for revenge. For mayhem—' He slammed his fist on the table and roared: 'Christ almighty, hasn't there been enough death today?'

Joe put his head in his hands. By this time, they both knew the kind of retaliation the Black and Tans and the Auxilaries had taken on innocent people. Now there was a stadium full of innocent men, women and children, out to see Dublin play Tipperary, eagerly looking forward to the match.

Michael stood up and began to pace backwards and forwards. His instinct was to go to Croke Park, to try to talk to the officials there, to do something to stop what was coming. He looked at his watch. It was probably already too late. The match was due to start in less than half an hour.

'What do you think, Joe?' he said. 'Should I go? Should I go to Croke Park?'

'Are you mad or what?' Joe looked horrified. 'You might as well walk up to the gates of Dublin Castle and tell them your name is Michael Collins and would they please take you in! It would be a crazy risk. You know very well that if you're caught, this whole house of cards – the spy network, the Squad, the arms supplies – the whole thing will collapse. In any case, if the Brits are going to take action, they are already on their way.'

Michael knew that Joe was right. He couldn't risk it. He was the one who controlled the lives and actions of so many of the men and women who were involved in the struggle. Sometimes it drove him crazy that he couldn't be the one to go hand-to-hand in battle, fight like a soldier, not lurk behind the scenes. Instead, he was hunted and hiding, day after day, night after night.

Why had he chosen today? It had seemed to make sense at the time: the crowds in Dublin for the match would make it easier for the assassins to escape. And he had been sure that the GAA would cancel the match as soon as they got his message and the news of the killings got out. What was wrong with people that they couldn't see what was in front of their noses? He felt sick to his stomach. Thousands of people would be at that match, at risk of death and injury.

Well, there was very little he could do for them. But perhaps he could do something about McKee, Clancy and Clune, the three young men who had been captured the previous evening. No-one had been able to find out where they were being held or what was happening to them. He stood up.

'I'm going out,' he said to Joe. 'You're right. I can't go to Croke Park and risk being captured. But I'm going to have a look nearby to see what's happening. Then I'll try to find out where our lads are being kept and maybe we can do something for them. We've managed to get people out of prison before now!'

As he cycled down the Drumcondra Road, he almost knocked down a man and two boys, dressed in the Dublin colours, rushing down the middle of the road as if the devil was after them. There was blood and what looked like tears streaming down the man's face. Michael hailed them, and they stopped, the man babbling:

'Don't go any nearer Croker; it's mayhem there. The Auxies just came rushing in and started firing at everybody.

We were near the gates so got out quick enough, but God help anyone who is caught in the middle of it. Look—'

Michael looked. There were streams of people coming from the direction of the stadium, many still sobbing and screaming. Some had blood on their clothes.

There had been carnage at Croke Park. The Auxilaries had fired into the crowd and killed fourteen civilians. They had injured dozens more, some badly. One of the players, the Tipperary full-back Mick Hogan, was shot dead as he crawled across the pitch, trying to escape the firing.

There was nothing he could do. Michael spent the rest of the afternoon frantically cycling across the city trying to get news of the prisoners. Nobody could say where they were or what was happening. Late in the evening, news came that the three prisoners had been shot 'while trying to escape'. Nobody believed that for a moment. Neligan sent reports that they had been held in the Castle and that the bodies of the young men showed signs of having been tortured before being killed.

Two of the young men had been Volunteers. Michael went to their funeral in the Pro-Cathedral. Many people thought he was crazy to show his face, on a day when the British forces could easily have captured him. But Michael was tired of hiding. He felt he owed it to his comrades to be there. If he was captured, he was captured. This was one of those days when he wondered if he cared whether he was captured or not.

While he was in the church, he said a prayer for all the other people who had died on that Sunday. He was not at all sure that he was going to be listened to. The Croke Park dead had included two boys, aged ten and eleven, and a young woman who had gone to the match with her fiancé. She had been due to get married the week after the massacre. Ordinary people, out to watch a match on a dark November day, had had their lives snuffed out, in a state of terror and anguish. When was it all going to end?

Dark Days

Dublin had become a ghost city. No-one wanted to risk going out in case they were caught up in the raids and shootings. Michael, on his trips across Dublin, had seen countless ordinary people being stopped and harassed by the Black and Tans and Auxiliaries. One incident in particular stuck in his memory. It happened during one of his early-morning cycles, close to some of the poorest tenements on the northside of the city. In these slum tenements, families of eight or ten or more lived crowded together in a single freezing room. Very little food, very little warmth, very little hygiene. People died in these rooms on a regular basis, children especially, babies most of all.

Michael slowed his bike down as he noticed a military lorry ahead of him, parked across the street. There was a child there too, carrying a billycan of milk, obviously on his way back from one of the dairies. The lorry of Auxies was blocking the child's way and he stood uncertainly while one of the men butted him with his rifle and sneered at him.

'Wotcha got in the can then, mate? Arms and ammunition, is it?'

'No, sir. Sure it's only milk for the baby, sir.'

'Milk for the baby? So he can grow up to be another dirty traitor and shoot at the armed forces?'

'No, sir. It's a girl.'

Perhaps the boy's voice had not been quite humble enough. Perhaps there had been a note of scorn in it. Perhaps not. It might just have been nerves. For whatever reason, it annoyed the Auxie; he tipped the billycan with his rifle, and the milk flowed over the pavement, splashing the boy's bare feet. The Auxie laughed and swung himself into the lorry, shouting at his companions to move on.

The boy stood, looking at his bare feet and the spilt milk. Michael could see how hard he was trying not to cry. He pushed his bike up to him.

'Arragh, don't be too upset. My mam always used to say there was no use crying over spilt milk.'

He smiled. The boy didn't smile back.

'But now the baby won't have any milk,' he said. 'And she's hungry, she's always hungry. That's why she cries all the time, me mam says.'

Michael felt in his pocket and handed the child a handful of coins. The boy's eyes lit up – he had hardly ever seen a silver coin before, never mind a bundle of them.

'Take that and get some more milk for the baby. And while you're at it, get your mammy to buy you some boots. With a bit of luck, the baby will grow up in a country where she won't have to be bothered about fighting the British army!'

He looked again at the child's feet, blue with cold, and added,

'And where both of you can have a decent pair of shoes on your feet. Don't worry, lad; we'll make it happen.'

Michael kept up the brave words. That was part of his job, to make people feel that it was all going to work out for the best. But he was wondering how long his luck could last.

* * *

At Christmas, stuck in Dublin, Michael invited some of his closest friends to dinner in the Gresham Hotel. There was no way he could make it down to Woodfield this year. The house was being watched all the time. He felt very bad about it, because Kathy, Johnnie's wife, was very ill. She had tuberculosis, the same terrible disease that had killed their first child, Michael, when he was only two years old. The Gresham dinner was meant to be a small escape from all his worries, but it didn't work out like that. The hotel was raided in the middle of the meal and Michael barely avoided being captured. It did make for a good story afterwards, especially when his dinner companions described how Michael had solemnly convinced one of the officers that the word 'rifles' scribbled in his notebook was actually 'refills'!

At the end of January, Kathy died, and a few weeks later, Johnnie was arrested. While he was in prison, a group of soldiers travelled out to Woodfield and burnt the house to the ground. Nancy made a trip down to see how the children were doing. She burst into tears when she described to Michael what she had found down there. She met him in Stephen's Green, and they sat watching the young ducklings on the pond. There was bright April sunshine but they hugged their coats tightly to them in the biting wind.

'It was awful, Michael. The walls are black ruins. You could still smell the smoke. I don't know if they will ever be able to rebuild it. The Essex Regiment made well sure it all went up. They forced the neighbours at gunpoint to set the fires. They burned the barn and most of the outhouses too.'

Nancy waited for Michael to use the phrase that she had heard him use so often: 'We'll make them pay.' But instead he said, 'They knew what would hurt me most. Where are the children now?'

'They're living in the little house that you were born in, Michael; the one that was being used as an outhouse. The soldiers didn't bother with that.'

Michael remembered his mother watching from the door of the big house as he left for London. He remembered sitting against her skirts at the wide hearth, listening to the stories of the ancient heroes. He remembered the house being built.

He had wanted to be a builder then. He had always wanted to build something. He had wanted to build a new country, but instead there was nothing but destruction all around him. Cork had been particularly hard hit by the Tans and the Auxies, mainly because the county was the most active in the rebellion. Cork city had been burnt in December – a revenge attack by the Auxiliaries. Some of them were still wearing burnt pieces of cork in their hats as a reminder to people of what they could do.

'Did you manage to see Johnnie?'

Nancy nodded and pulled her coat tighter against the wind.

'Yes, just a short visit. It's very hard on him – first Kathy dying and now this ... But he told me to tell you to keep up the work! He gave me the same message for the children.'

'How are they?'

'Ah, they're brave children; the cousins and the neighbours are keeping an eye on them and the older ones are minding the small ones. But they still have nightmares about it, and they have lost everything. The soldiers didn't allow them to take anything out of the house.'

She gave a little laugh that turned into a sob.

'The children told me that the soldiers came and drank up all the milk from the dairy. Oh, Michael, what would your mother have felt! At least she's not alive to see this. It would have broken her heart. All the work wasted.'

'We have to make sure the work isn't wasted,' said Michael grimly. 'I promise you this: I'll make sure it isn't.'

'How are things going?' Nancy was speaking very quietly now. She was cautious about asking Michael questions like this. These days you could have your head bitten off in a moment if you said the wrong thing. But today he seemed eager to talk.

He made a face. 'It's not getting any easier. Some of our ways of getting ammunition and guns have been blocked.'

'At least Dev brought a lot of money from America.'

'The money's not much use if there's nowhere to get the arms.'

'Are you glad he's back?'

'Ah, sure it's better he is. He needs to be here. But he really doesn't have much of a clue about how to fight this war. He wants big dramatic battles, and I'm telling you that it's the guerrilla stuff that works.'

'Well, the escape from Kilmainham must have made him happy.'

'Yes, those three lads getting out hit all the papers. And we've had a few smaller victories – every little thing counts. Did you know that the laundries are refusing to take in clothes from the army? So that's another thorn in their side. And Crossbarry was a great victory. Our county is doing more than its share.'

'And how is it up north?' Nancy asked.

'The news from there is not so good, I'm sorry to say. The

Unionists are attacking anyone they think might want to be part of the revolution. They have their own parliament now, and that will make it harder to try to draw them into our new state.'

'What's Dev's take on it all?'

'He says that there are noises coming over from London about some kind of truce or compromise. But he won't deal with anyone except Lloyd George.'

'Well, he *is* the Prime Minister.'

'Yes, he's right too. We need to know that whatever is agreed is agreed at the very top.'

'Would you like to see a truce?' asked Nancy.

'Would I what? I'm sick of the killing and looking at villages burnt, homes destroyed. I've seen enough buildings on fire and enough bodies laid out to last me a lifetime!'

'You must be happy that Harry is back, at least.'

'I am. But to tell you the truth, Nancy, things are different. We're not as close as we used to be.'

'Is it to do with Kitty?'

'A bit. But it's to do with Dev, too.'

'There's always been a bit of competition between you and Dev, hasn't there?'

Michael shrugged. 'I suppose so. Not that I grudge him the speech-making and the politics. He's a better politician than I ever will be. But I get tired of him thinking he knows anything

141

about how this war can be won ... Dev is many things, but he's no military genius. And I don't think he trusts me. To be honest, I'm not sure who I trust myself these days. Things are worse with Cathal Brugha and Austin Stack than they have ever been. There's nothing but rows with my so-called comrades.'

'The strain is hard on everyone. You know you can be very hard too, Michael, too blunt. Criticising other people's work because it doesn't meet your high standards. Hurting their feelings. Maybe you need to stock up on bull's-eyes?'

Michael gave a short laugh. 'It's a far cry from bull's-eyes and serenades we are these days. As for hurting their feelings—'

Michael kicked at a stone in frustration. It fell into the pond and scared off the little group of ducklings who had been gathered at the edge.

'What's a few hurt feelings when there's a bloody war going on? Do you know how many people have died since Christmas? Over three hundred, maybe more.'

Nancy said nothing and Michael stood up.

'We'd better get moving before we're spotted. It was good to get the news, Nancy. Thanks for that. And you're right about my temper. You might not believe it, but I am really trying to control it these days!'

* * *

Michael slammed his fist on the table. It was the end of May and the smoke from the burning Custom House still drifted from the ruins of the beautiful building on the quays. For days, scraps of ancient documents had floated through the air and gently landed on the quay walls or on the surface of the Liffey.

'I told you it would be a disaster.'

Dev looked at him over the top of his round spectacles.

'It was no such thing,' he said in a mild voice. 'We have discussed this already, Michael. I told you the shootings by snipers and the raids do not look good in the eyes of the world. We need to be seen to be fighting a real war, with clean battles. The Custom House attack was that – it was a legitimate target, with all the British records held there. It's a public relations success. All the papers have reported it, and not just in Ireland and England.'

'That's all very well, but there are five of the Dublin battalion dead and eighty men captured. That's nearly everyone who was involved in the attack! We're throwing away men that are needed! And now Dublin has yet another ruin to add to its collection.'

'Michael, you opposed this attack in the Cabinet and you were overruled. There was a democratic decision to go ahead. This is not a military dictatorship here.'

'Yes, I accepted it. But the Cabinet was wrong! I'm the one who knows most about military matters! No-one else has a clue!'

'You are not the Minister of Defence; Cathal Brugha is. You are not even the head of the army.'

'As Cathal tells me every time he meets me! Himself and Austin Stack are both useless at their jobs, Dev, and you know it.'

'It is not my job to take sides, Michael. And you don't take it at all well yourself when other people interfere with your business. Don't think I don't know about all those files with DBI written on the front of them. *Don't Butt In!* Some people have christened you Mr Don't Butt In! Yet you have no problem butting into other people's business.'

'I can't stand seeing people making a mess of things ... and I don't like being called names – like Don't Butt In and Mickeen!'

'We have both been called many names. I am sure there have been times when your names for me may have been even less polite! As for the quality of their work, that's just your opinion. You do tend to be one of those people who always think they can do a better job than anyone else. But you need to respect your colleagues in the Dáil. Austin and Cathal are both strong, principled men. I fought with Cathal in 1916 and saw his courage. I have never seen anything like it!'

'Nobody is questioning their courage or their sincerity, Dev, just their ability! And I would remind you that I am the one who will have to try to replace the arms and ammunition lost in your Custom House adventure. Not to mention the soldiers.'

Truce!

The country erupted in joy. De Valera had played his cards close to his chest. Michael was not included in the very secret talks that went on that summer. But by July there was a meeting of the Cabinet where Dev made his announcement.

'Truce! Truce!' The newspaper boys were shouting their heads off but they didn't need to. People were grabbing the newspapers out of their hands, hardly able to believe the great news. De Valera had managed to get Lloyd George to agree to meetings. They would discuss the demands of the self-declared Irish government. For the first time in hundreds of years, it looked as if the independence of Ireland was a real possibility. In the meantime, the Black and Tans and the Auxilaries would be taken off the streets and the Republican Army would stop its raids and ambushes and assassinations.

Dublin went crazy. Some people walked around the city as if in a dream, hardly able to believe that there were no more armoured cars on the roads. Instead, the trams were lit up and began to travel late in the evening. People blew tin trumpets and waved flags and lit bonfires. Some sang and danced in the streets, staying out until the early hours of the morning, just because they could. No more curfew! No more searches every time you went out in the city. There was no more gunfire from passing lorries, no more snipers hiding in the shadows. No more fear of being caught in the crossfire and killed.

Michael breathed a sigh of relief. No-one but he knew how low their supplies of ammunition and guns were. They could not have kept up the battle much longer, especially with Dev's demands for big dramatic gestures like the Custom House attack. Maybe, just maybe, this war was coming to an end. The old story of defeat and sorrow could end and a new story could be written. But first there would have to be the talks about an agreement. The decision was made to send a delegation to London to discuss a treaty between the two countries. Michael was called into De Valera's office.

'I want you to be one of the delegates going over to London.'

'Dev, you know I'm not a diplomat! I'm the last person you should be sending over for this kind of negotiation.'

'Michael, you were furious with me because I didn't let you get involved in the earlier meetings. Now I am telling you I want you to be involved in these ones. I cannot see that you should have a problem with this.'

'But you were there too for the earlier meetings, and now you say you're not going to go over to London for these ones!'

'I will stay here and you will report back to me. There will be a good balance, between you and the other delegates. Arthur Griffith will lead the delegation and hold everyone steady.'

'No, I'm telling you, I'm not going to go. You should be the one going over!'

'It is my decision, Michael, and I think, politically, it would be better for me to stay here. You will have plenipotentiary powers.'

'What the Hell are they?'

Dev took out his pipe. It was never lit as he didn't approve of smoking, but when he took it out of his mouth, it usually meant a lecture was on the way. *Now I've done it*, thought Michael. There was nothing Dev liked more than giving Michael lectures. But this time, Dev's lecture was surprisingly short.

'You can discuss matters with the British government and decide if what they offer is acceptable. Then the offer will have to be ratified by us here. I want you to keep me closely informed of every suggested change or nuance in what is being discussed or agreed.'

Michael looked at the leader of the country sourly. Dev didn't really need Michael to report back. He was sure that he was going to be well informed of what went on in the negotiations. Erskine Childers, the Secretary of the delegation, would report everything back directly to Dev. Well, there was one thing for sure: Michael was not going to stay in the same building as the other delegates and have every move he made watched. Arthur Griffith had always been a bit too cautious for Michael's taste. Michael was friendly with Robert Barton but Erskine Childers was his cousin and they were very close. These days ... these days, it was hard to trust anyone.

'If I go to London, I will be seen in public. There will be photographs taken. That was the reason you gave for not bringing me to the earlier meetings. You said the fact that no-one knew what I looked like made it too big a risk to have me photographed, that my cover would be blown if we had to go back to war. What's changed now?'

'Things have moved on,' said Dev.

'You do know I can never be safe again, if the negotiations fail?'

'Then you will just have to make sure that they do not fail,' said Dev calmly.

Michael almost slammed the door behind him as he left the office, but stopped himself in time. A slammed door wasn't going to make any difference to what Dev had decided. What he had really wanted to do in that office was wrestle De Valera to the ground and possibly bite his ears, ears that stuck out as if just waiting to be pulled. He snorted with laughter. Yes, he was being childish but he would have loved to see the Long

Fella's face if he had gone for him. He started to walk furiously towards Vaughan's Hotel, where he was hoping to meet Harry.

* * *

'Well, apart from the beginning, I mostly kept my cool. I've learned that it doesn't pay to let the Long Fella know that he has made you red roaring mad. Though I still feel red roaring mad, and here I am being sent to discuss the future of Ireland with some of the wiliest foxes in the world! He's landing me in it on purpose. I can't win. We are never going to get everything we ask for, and then I'll be the bad guy who failed, who didn't get what we wanted. Is it that he's jealous of me? Look at the way he wanted me to go to America, just as soon as he came back. He was all for getting me out of the way. Joe O'Reilly suggested that to me, and he isn't the only one who thought so.'

Harry was silent for a moment.

'It is possible there's a bit of that. But are you sure there's not a bit of jealousy on your side as well, Michael? You always want to win, you know, whether it's a match or an argument!'

Michael slammed his fist on the table.

'Jealous of him? That miserable drip of a man?'

'Michael, he's a lot more than that, and you know it.'

Michael's head jerked, as it always did when he was very upset.

'Arragh, I suppose he is.'

149

'In any case, there's no need for jealousy,' Harry continued. 'You are the dashing hero, he's the schoolmaster in people's eyes. And he admits that himself, Mick. Hasn't he often said to us, "Bear with me, I am only an old schoolmaster?"'

'So you agree! He wouldn't mind seeing me take a fall.'

'Neither of you would mind seeing the other one take a fall, but that doesn't mean Dev is setting you up for one. You two are very different, but in some ways you are very alike! Maybe it's because you're from the same country background and you both lost your fathers when you were young!'

'We are not alike at all! My family were strong farmers – I never had to graze the cows on the side of the road like Dev did! And I didn't get sent home to be brought up by relatives while my mother worked in America, miles away from me!'

'Yes, Mick, you were luckier in your childhood. That doesn't mean that you were any better.'

Michael looked a little ashamed.

'You're right, Harry. I shouldn't be gloating over my good fortune. But at the same time, Dev got the education – I was working from the time I was fourteen, so the luck wasn't all one way.'

'Ah, Mick, you had a family to help you and love you!'

'Dev has a wife and children now! Those children are great and Sinéad is a woman in a million! What have I got? I haven't even got a roof to call my own in the middle of all this mess!

And now Dev wants to use me as a scapegoat! Admit it, Harry, you've practically said he wants me to fail.'

Harry stood up.

'That's not what I said. I'm not going to listen to that kind of talk about the Chief. He has brought us this far, hasn't he? You used to respect his judgement. You should still respect it. You're going to have to trust him, Mick.'

Back in London

ondon again, but this was a very different trip from any of the others Michael had made. He didn't travel over with the rest of the delegates. He came a day later as he had family business to attend to – buying an engagement ring for Kitty. She had finally made up her mind. She had committed herself to marrying Michael. They planned to get married the following June. That was, if they all managed to survive until then and the country wasn't still in chaos. And Michael wasn't back on the run.

The press were disappointed not to see Michael arrive with the other delegates, but they made up for it when they went together to the first meeting in Downing Street. The street was filled with crowds eager to see the glamorous and elusive Mr Collins. Cheering men, women and children; some clergy even, singing hymns and reciting the rosary. Banners with good luck wishes in Irish; tricolours everywhere.

The Irish in London had come out of hiding. Reporters were everywhere, photographers and film crews, all trying to catch a glimpse of the man who had escaped capture for so long. In the newspapers, he seemed to have gained magical powers of escape and invisibility. Michael thought he would like to sneak into a cinema and watch a newsreel, just to see what the comments would be. He could hardly do it himself, but he might ask Kitty to do it for him.

Despite the fact that he had not wanted to come to London, Michael was determined to do all he could to get the best deal possible for Ireland. This was the most important piece of work he would ever have to do, and he would do his very best to make it a success.

There were going to be sticking points. For a start, it was obvious that the British would not want to agree to a full republic. They would want to keep Ireland in some way connected to the British Crown, like their dominions across the seas.

Then there was the question of the north of Ireland, the northeast section of the country that had already been granted its own parliament in Belfast. The majority of people in that part of Ireland still wanted to stay connected to Britain. For decades, they had not even wanted a separate parliament in Dublin. One of their slogans had been 'Home Rule means Rome Rule' – they were sure that the Roman Catholic south would be controlled by its bishops and priests. Most of the northerners were Protestant and were horrified at the very thought of this.

The northeast was also much more prosperous than most of the south of Ireland, and many of the people who lived there did not want to be connected with people they considered lazy, backward and poor. Nobody could deny that the divide existed, but it went against all the ideals of a republic to put it into law. To divide the country between north and south would mean selling out the nationalist Catholics who lived there. So how could they come to some kind of arrangement that everyone could sign up to? The next few weeks were going to be very tough.

They were tougher than Michael could have imagined. As the days went on, he felt that he was caught in some kind of nightmare. Talk and talk and more talk. Round and round in circles, with the same points made again and again. He often thought he would far rather be on the run in Dublin, broken ribs and all, rather than walk into the beautiful, lavish conference room one more time. He had got to know every inch of the elaborate plaster on the ceiling, every cupid and wreath of flowers. He had spent so much time looking up at it as one or other of the delegation talked on and on.

One good result of all the meetings was that he and Arthur Griffith had got to know each other better. He had always respected Griffith, though he did not agree with all his politics. And he had never been sure of what Arthur Griffith thought of him. They were very different, but as the negotiations went on, they both realised that the other was totally sincere about doing his very best for Ireland. Apart from this growing friendship, though, the Irish delegation did not get on well together. That didn't help them negotiate very well.

Between all the meetings, Michael was invited to dinners and the theatre and concerts. He spent a lot of time with John and Hazel Lavery. Hazel was a popular society hostess – a job in itself in those days. John Lavery was a famous painter, and he painted a portrait of Michael, who he complained was very difficult to paint as he never sat still! Michael had also made new friends in London, and even met one of his heroes – J.M. Barrie, the man who had written Peter Pan.

As he sat through some of the fabulous dinners in the great houses of London society, his mind went back to the stories told at the forge, so very long ago: tales of landlords feasting in London while the Irish peasants starved. Well, there was an Irish peasant at the table now. Sometimes it went to his head; some of the meals ended up with Michael's usual horseplay disrupting the nice, civilised dinners!

One of his main escapes from all the stress was walks with Hannie, who was still working in the Post Office. He sometimes went with her to Kensington Gardens. On one foggy November day, Hannie paused their walk at the statue of Peter Pan.

'You know, Michael, when you left London, you were a bit of a Peter Pan yourself. You still had not totally grown up. Still a bit of a wild lad!'

'And now?'

'Apart from the odd report of you throwing nuts at people at the dinner table, you've changed, Michael.'

'Well, my suits are a lot better than they used to be!'

'Be serious now. Can you not see it yourself?'

'Maybe I lose my temper a bit less. But I still lose it far too often!'

'Ah, you still have a bit of that awful temper, that's true. And a streak of your old devilment! You will never lose that. But you're a man now. No, it's more than that. I really admire the way that you're dealing with all the madness here. The crowds, the newspapermen following you—'

Michael laughed.

'Did I tell you about the one who told me that I should go to the States? He said I could make quite a big stir there! I told him I thought I was making quite a big stir here already!'

Hannie laughed too.

'No, I hadn't heard that story. But well done for not letting it go to your head. You don't care if they call you a great Irish hero, or an ignorant Mick, or even "a quite agreeable savage"! I loved your answer to that newspaper man who asked you how it felt to be a great man.'

'Well, it's true – how would I know? In any case, I have you and Kitty to keep me from losing the run of myself. I wouldn't want to be seen to be wasting my energy on all that rubbish. I have a job to do.'

'Yes, and you are doing it. You're not just a soldier or a politician now, Michael. You are a statesman.'

For once, Michael did not brush off the compliment with a laugh or a joke. He gave his slow smile and said, 'I'm only doing what our mother reared us to do. I'm trying to get the job finished. And Hannie, more than anything else, I want to get this done and over with and get home.'

'Be careful when you do get home, Michael. They may turn against you yet!'

'I know I'll be facing a battle in Dublin, Hannie. But if we see it through, it will all be worth it.'

He thought of the little donkey, of the white roads leading through the hills at Granard and at Sam's Cross. Of being in a quiet place with Kitty, a place with trees and birdsong. There were days now when he felt more imprisoned than he ever had at Frongoch.

* * *

By December, it was obvious that the British were never going to agree to a republic and that the north of Ireland, in some form or other, was going to remain attached to the United Kingdom. Fighting had got worse among the Irish delegates. The others resented the fact that, at many of the meetings, only Arthur Griffith and Michael Collins were present.

On 6 December, a treaty was finally signed. It gave Ireland Dominion status, which meant that it was still attached to

Britain. Anyone who took government office would also have to swear loyalty to the Crown. The hardest part for Michael to accept was the part about the north. Northern Ireland would cut itself off from what was to be called the Free State of Ireland. There would be a boundary commission set up to create a permanent border between the two parts of the country.

Some of the other delegates, especially Erskine Childers, railed against the Treaty, particularly because the new Ireland would not be the Republic they had fought for. Michael and Arthur Griffith argued that they were never going to get the British to agree to a republic at this stage. This agreement would give virtual independence to Ireland, and over time they could work to get a full and free republic,

'It's the freedom to get freedom,' Michael said to his companions.' And it's as good as we are ever going to get from this crowd. They're already saying that they will end the truce if we don't agree to this final offer. And if the truce ends, it'll be all-out war, I'm telling you, and we won't be able to fight against them. We will have lost our power to act secretly. And even more important – we will have lost the goodwill of the Irish people. That support is the only thing that has kept the struggle going. And now the Irish people want peace.'

'But to swear loyalty to the British king! That's against the oath we took to fight for the Republic!'

Robert Barton was clenching his fists in frustration.

Arthur Griffith, pale and tired, spoke quietly: 'This is independence by any other name. This is more than I dreamed of when I founded Sinn Féin, and I am willing to sign. So is Michael.'

Erskine Childers shrugged.

'Right so. But I'm telling you that Dev will not be one bit happy about this.'

The Treaty

Christmas was over. It had not been a good one for Michael. When the delegates arrived back with the news that the Treaty had been signed, Dev exploded.

'Could you not even have telephoned me before you signed?'

Griffith tried to explain that they didn't know where he was.

'Then you should have waited! You should have come back and checked with us here … you should have checked with me!'

'I thought you told us we were plenipotentiaries!'

'That doesn't mean you could just sign for us all! I am the President. And as for the oath of allegiance: you have sold out the heroes of 1916! And you have also sold out the Catholics in the north.'

'The border is already there, Dev,' said Michael. 'The parliament is set up already.'

'Yes, but it shouldn't be! One third of the people there don't agree with it. Well, we shall present this – this travesty – to the Dáil. But I will be telling people to vote against it!'

Debates on the Treaty started before Christmas. Most of the deputies promised at the beginning of their speeches that they would be brief, and then went on for what felt like forever and in some cases really was hours. Through it all, Michael kept quiet and reined in his temper. He held tight to one idea: he would get people to work together for unity in the Dáil and in the army. That was the important thing. They couldn't afford the risk of more violence and bloodshed. Michael knew very well how easily violence could erupt again. There would be more people killed and injured, more homes burnt to the ground. More lives destroyed. He put the case that there should be an effort made by everyone to work together, to keep the peace and set up the structures that would make the new Ireland. But many people did not want to listen to him.

It was decided that the Dáil vote on whether the Treaty would be accepted would be held after Christmas. Michael hoped that this would give people a chance to think and also give those who were most against the Treaty time to calm down.

He was also desperately tired. He managed to spend a few days in Woodfield over Christmas, and saw Johnnie and the children. He and Johnnie walked through the blackened ruins of the family home. Ivy was tangling itself around the hearth, where the fire had been kept lighted for over twenty years, the warm centre of the house. Nature had already begun to take back the stone. *Nature and time make all things equal and all things beautiful in the end*, thought Michael. *Slowly but surely, the wounds people make on the landscape are healed. Maybe time even heals the wounds humans make on each other, in the end.* He talked to Johnnie about the need to keep unity in the Dáil.

'Even if the ones who don't agree with us can just come along with the agreement for a while, I'm sure over time we can get a better deal. I can't stand the thought of fighting against men and women who were like brothers and sisters to me.'

'You've come a long way, Michael! The lad who always wanted a scrap trying to avoid one at all costs!'

'That's because I have seen the results of the endless scrapping, and I have had enough of it.'

* * *

Michael looked around him; this was the red letter day, 7 January 1921. The day the vote would to be taken. People had spoken passionately for and against the agreement. Michael had given a speech from the heart. He said he would accept the decision of the Dáil if the Treaty was not passed. But he saw the Treaty as a stepping stone to freedom. Then he tried his best to stay silent while insults were hissed at him and men and women he had looked on as friends turned away when he tried to meet their eye. There were moments of humour, and moments when the old comradeship shone through.

Harry, to Michael's intense disappointment, had sided with Dev against the Treaty. He and Michael, now on opposite sides of the debate, carefully addressed each other as 'my friend' during the Dáil sessions, but they both knew that their friendship was becoming threadbare.

Through it all, Michael kept calm, finding patience inside himself that he had never realised he had. He did not respond when some people, like Cathal Brugha, used the debates to attack him. Cathal Brugha had been furious to hear Griffith describe Michael as the man who had won the war. In response, he had tried to make little of all the work Michael had done, and had even insulted him personally. He mocked the fact that Michael had been the organiser of the raids and skirmishes, rather than leading them himself. Michael didn't let himself show any anger.

But it was hard to say nothing when he was accused of selling out the dream of Pearse and Connolly, the heroes he had fought with in the GPO. The worst of it was, he wasn't sure that there wasn't an element of truth in what people said. He felt especially bad that Ireland was going to be split. He was afraid that the Catholic nationalists in the north would be treated as second-class citizens. They might even be attacked. Catholics had been killed and hundreds burned out of their homes before now.

The votes were counted: 57 against the Treaty; 64 for the Treaty. The Treaty had been passed.

There was uproar. Dev, looking twenty years older than he had before Christmas, started to say something, then stopped abruptly. He covered his face with his hands to hide the tears that were streaming down his face.

The following Monday, the Dáil met again. De Valera refused to be part of the new government. Michael suggested Arthur Griffith as the new President of Dáil Éireann. Dev walked out of the chamber. Michael's heart sank when he saw Harry follow him. Many more left too, shouting insults at those who were left behind, who replied with more insults.

'Traitors!'

Constance Markievicz gave him a filthy look as she prepared to follow Dev. During the debates, she had already made a few snide suggestions that Michael had somehow been bribed by the British. So now, when he saw the Countess leaving the Dáil, he couldn't help shouting out:

'Deserters all!'

'Oath breakers and cowards!' Constance shouted back.

'Foreigners ... Americans ... English!'

'Lloyd Georgeites!'

This has to be the lowest point I have ever reached, thought Michael. *This is what it's like when the people turn on you. This should be a great day for Ireland.*

Instead, it felt like the worst day of his life.

Brother Against Brother

No-one was quite sure what was going to happen next. De Valera's followers grouped together to make a second cabinet. There was to be an election held in June to see which group would be elected by the people. Both Dev and Michael tried to keep things from going from bad to worse. They arranged meetings. Sometimes Harry acted as the go-between.

The last of these meetings was held in one of the safe houses that had been used by both Harry and Michael through the years they had fought together. The two men met in the dining room, a chilly room with a small coal fire and a picture of the Virgin Mary over the mantelpiece. The room smelled of cabbage and beeswax. They looked at each other across the polished table and talked about what could be done to reach some kind of compromise.

Nobody raised their voice, nobody slammed their fist on the table, nobody shook hands. The meeting didn't go on for very long as it was clear that no agreement was going to be found. The best that could be agreed was that, before the coming election, there would be no violence on the part of the army that did not accept the Treaty, and no arrests by the Provisional Government. Michael was now the Leader of the Provisional Government. Harry was no longer a Dáil deputy.

They stared at each other in silence and then Harry stood up.

'I still can't believe you accepted this deal, Mick. That you have sold out on the Republic and on our people in the north. That you have agreed to an oath of loyalty to the English king!'

'It's not a sell-out, Harry. It's a step towards getting the Republic. And it's a huge step. Can you not see that? How many times do I have to explain? Can we not just put it to the people of Ireland and see what they want?'

'I think you were brainwashed while you were in England. Look, Mick, this isn't going anywhere. You can't push me into agreeing with you this time. I think I might as well head off.'

'You're right. Just as a matter of interest, though, Harry, what did you do with the Russian jewels?'

Harry's face grew red.

'The ones the Bolsheviks gave as security for the loan we made them? The ones you threw at me because you said there was blood on them? They are hidden well, as well or better than you could hide them, Mick. I'll give them back to the Dáil on the day the Republic is declared!'

Michael said nothing. Harry left the room.

Michael sat staring at the picture of the Virgin Mary with her arms outstretched. They had had the same picture in the parlour in Woodfield. He knew the figure in the picture was meant to give comfort, but to him it looked as if she was giving up in despair. He knew how that felt. He continued to stare, listening to Harry's footsteps as his friend walked away from him down the hallway. He heard the front door open and close.

During the next few months, Michael campaigned hard. He travelled all over the country, giving passionate speeches to huge crowds. He also spent hours chatting to everyone and anyone, smiling and joking and listening with sympathy to people's problems. Convict 242 and Michael's new puppy, Danny Boy, became the best-travelled dogs in Ireland.

Arthur Griffith was now President of the Dáil, but Michael was still the Leader of the Provisional Government so he did most of the practical work of organising the campaign and the British withdrawal. He felt exhausted most of the time, and suffered a lot from pains in his stomach. He wondered if the pain was caused by something more than just stress, but he didn't want to go to a doctor. There were times when he felt so low that he didn't care if the worst happened. Kitty tried her best to support him, but Michael was now a very different person from the carefree boy she had met in 1917. Still, she stopped him thinking non-stop about politics by talking about their plans for the future, and she even managed to make him laugh sometimes. Their wedding was postponed from June to a date in the autumn, when they would have a joint wedding with Maud and Gearóid. Granard was still a haven for Michael, and he got there as often as he could, though not as often as he would have liked.

One of these visits made him late for what was one of the most important days in Irish history, the day that the British administration left Dublin Castle. It took place on a cold day in January. There was a special ceremony and the tricolour was raised. Thousands of people lined up to see the Castle finally in the hands of an Irish government. Michael was almost two hours late as the train from Granard was delayed. It didn't stop him smiling and laughing as he looked around the building that had been the centre of British rule for centuries. The crowds cheered and cheered, as if their lungs would burst.

As he left the Castle yard, Michael thought he saw someone he recognised. Surely that young boy in the flat cap was the one he had given the money to, the day the child had had his can of milk kicked over? He smiled and waved at him, and the boy, who was carrying a little girl in his arms, smiled and held up his sister's arm so she could wave a tricolour back at Michael.

Michael wrote to Kitty that evening that he was as happy a man as there was in Ireland that day.

He tried to remember those happy moments. There were not many of them.

* * *

In April, he entered his office and saw by Joe's face that something terrible had happened.

'Well, Joe, what is it now? Bad news again?'

Michael spoke quietly. He rarely, if ever, roared his questions or tried to wrestle people to the floor any more.

Joe nodded. 'About as bad as it can be, Mick. Some of the anti-Treaty lads have taken over the Four Courts.'

Most of the army had accepted the Treaty, many of them saying that if it was good enough for the Big Fella, it was good enough for them. But others sided with the anti-Treaty deputies and were quite prepared to fight for their ideal of a 32-county republic.

Michael said nothing for a moment. He stood up and shoved his hands into his pockets, hiding his clenched fists.

He began to pace around the room.

'Bloody eejits! Who is leading them?'

'Rory O'Connor. There's about 200 of them.'

Michael walked to the window, his hands still in his pockets.

'They're hoping we'll react, or the British will react, and that'll be the end of the Treaty. It'll be more mayhem and shooting.'

He stood looking out the window at the blue April sky.

'The boyos in London will be putting pressure on me to do something. But I won't. Rory was one of the best of our men. They are our lads still. They are eejits. But they're our own eejits.'

Dev and Michael tried to make a pact between them so that the Treaty would not become an issue in the June election, but it soon broke down. The main result of the pact was that Arthur Griffith was furious with Michael and started to call him Mr Collins again. In the end, the deputies supporting the Treaty were voted in a by a huge majority in the election of June 1922, but only a couple of weeks afterwards, things went from bad to worse. The government was put under heavy pressure from Britain to do something about the Four Courts siege. Troops were sent in.

The Provisional Government defeated the anti-Treaty soldiers in the battle of the Four Courts, but at the cost of a great many lives. The building was also destroyed, and thousands of records, hundreds of years old, were turned to ashes. History was made that day, but even more history was destroyed. For days on end, the building smoked, and scraps of paper and parchment drifted into the air. Michael thought of all the history, all the work, all going up in flames. So many things lost. Cork burning. The Customs House blazing. Woodfield a black ruin. Photographs, papers, the cloak belonging to his grandmother. All burnt and lost.

'Woodfield was my memory,' he said to Kitty. 'This was the country's memory. We can never replace them. Some things that are lost can never be regained. Like my friendship with Harry.'

Battles continued in Dublin. Cathal Brugha was part of a siege in the Gresham Hotel. He left the blazing building, his pistol raised, and was killed. Michael was part of an army again, and had taken on the role of Commander-in-Chief. For the first time since the Rising, he dressed in an army uniform. Now he was fighting against the men and women he had fought with only a few months before. It made him sick to his stomach. In his home county, resistance to the Treaty was especially strong. People continued to be killed. Houses and businesses continued to be burned to the ground. And in the north of Ireland, there was mayhem.

Every week brought more bad news. In early August, Arthur Griffith died. Then Harry Boland was killed, shot while an attempt was being made to arrest him. Michael wrote to Kitty: 'Whatever use my prayers and thoughts are, he has them. I'd send a wreath only they would probably send it back torn up.'

He did make sure that a soldier from the government army was there to give the salute when Harry was buried.

Throughout the summer, the situation in the north had got worse. There were families in Catholic areas being driven out of their homes, told to go down to the south with the rest of the Fenians. Michael secretly organised to send arms to protect them. By doing this, he was breaking the agreement with London that the Irish Free State would not interfere in the affairs of the north. It was a very dangerous thing to do, as it put the Treaty at risk. But Michael could not look on as people – people he thought of as his people – were being attacked. In any case, there was very little he could do. He was still trying to get better terms from the British, in the hope that there might be enough progress made to win over the people who were against the Treaty. He knew himself, as he had known from the beginning, that the agreement was not perfect.

He took even less rest than he had when he had been on the run. All the people who loved Michael – his family and Kitty and Joe – worried about him. In fact, Joe's fussing put Michael into a rage at times. But Joe didn't care when Michael raged at him. He was afraid that his leader's health would break down, and he would do anything he could to stop that happening, even if it meant getting shouted at and having things thrown at him.

As the summer of 1922 began to draw to a close, nobody could say what would happen next.

The Way to the Pasture

'Will you rebuild the house?'

Johnnie sighed. 'I don't think I have the heart to. We'll do a bit of work on the old house. Maybe it's better that it's gone. Kathy always said she thought there were TB germs in the very walls of it. To be honest, Michael, the heart is gone out of the place. And there's a lot of bitterness around.'

Michael was on a trip to west Cork. The tour was an official one, but he had also used the journey for some unofficial business. He had met some of his old comrades and had talked about ways and means that might help to sort out the mess. There had been some rays of light, some hope that there might be an end to the violence and division. There might yet be a peaceful way forward for the country.

Now he was in Sam's Cross, where he had stopped to meet some of his old friends and his relatives. Johnnie had

MICHAEL COLLINS

come over from Woodfield to meet him in their cousins' house. Across the road, the rest of the men in the convoy were enjoying a drink in the pub. Michael and Johnnie were having a few minutes alone together.

Michael had passed Woodfield on his journey but had not had time to stop at the house. As he passed the farm, he remembered the days when he had played there with his brothers and sisters, and he allowed himself to dream a little. He dreamt of children as noisy and wild as he and his brothers and sisters had been. Children with Kitty's eyes and her smile of pure mischief. And of course there would be Kerry Blues, and ponies and chickens. Surely, someday soon, he would be allowed to have an ordinary life? Maybe by the time October came, and he and Kitty were married, things might have become quieter.

He pulled his attention back to Johnnie. His brother was asking him: 'How did the meetings go?'

'I don't want to hope too much, but you know, Johnnie, not too badly. There might be a bit of light at the end of the tunnel.'

'What about Dev?'

'Dev? I don't know. To be honest, a lot of the lads fighting on the ground won't pay any heed to what he says. And they are the ones who will keep the battle going.'

'And a lot of them will want to. People around here won't

give up the ideal of the Republic too easily'!

'We aren't asking them to give up their ideals. Just their arms! I don't want any more fighting and burning and killing. I just want a bit of peace so we can get the country moving again. We can all work towards the Republic together then. I am going to put an end to this bloody war if it's the last thing I do!'

'I hope you can do it, but it will be some job. People have already got very stuck in their ideas. Listen, do you think there's a chance that you'll make it down again to us when Hannie comes over in a couple of weeks? We could try to get Katie and her husband to come down too and have a family reunion!'

'I'll try my very best, Johnnie, but I can't promise anything at the moment. Believe me, there's nothing I'd like better than to spend some time here with you all. I'd love to bring Kitty down to see the place. One of my dreams is to spend a couple of months just wandering around the countryside, getting to know people and seeing something more of it than I've seen from the back of a campaign lorry. But there's so much to be done, and at the moment we can't be sure of anything.'

'Aye, that's true. You can't trust anyone either. Be sure to be careful on the way back to Cork. Use the armoured car. Every move you make is being watched!'

'Sam's Cross hasn't changed a bit then! We never used to be able to get away with anything! But surely they won't try to shoot me in my own county!'

He stood up. Johnnie stood too, and looked keenly at his brother.

'Don't take this badly, but you don't look well. How is your health?'

'Ah, I know I've got fat and lazy.'

'Never lazy, Michael, never lazy. Maybe you have put on some weight but it's more than that. Your eyes are sunk into your head!'

'That's only the lack of sleep. And I've a bit of a cold. Don't start fussing now, Johnnie; I have enough of that with Joe. He made me drink hot orange juice last night! Hot orange juice! I think he would have tucked me into bed if I hadn't roared at him to get away to hell outa that!'

Johnnie didn't laugh.

'We all know that you're a terrible patient. I don't know how Joe puts up with you. But your stomach? Hannie said you were having problems. Have you been to see a doctor?'

'Sure I haven't time to go to a doctor.'

'You're like our mother. She didn't go to one either.'

'I'm grand, I'm telling you.'

'You'll kill yourself, Michael.'

Already halfway out the door, Michael turned back to Johnnie.

'People have been telling me I'll kill myself for years.' He gave his brother his biggest smile. 'And look at me. I'm not dead yet.'

* * *

The light slanted, flickered as they drove through the darkening green of trees and bushes. Just outside Bandon, they stopped briefly so that Michael could say hello to a Kerry Blue terrier who was being taken for a walk by his owner. Now the car trundled through the quiet lanes. Some of the harvest still stood tall and golden, but it would soon be cut.

Dog daisies in the ditches, and the hedges showing early blackberries, red and purple. There were three little girls picking them. Their laughter and the song of a single blackbird were the only sounds breaking the silence, apart from the noise of the convoy. Michael closed his eyes and remembered the hours he had spent gathering berries. The blackberry jams and tarts were always best when mixed with the apples from the orchard. *This is Ireland*, thought Michael. *This is what I am fighting for.* Ferns high as bushes, fuchsia like drops of blood against the dark green. The edges of the hedgerow leaves that had become ragged with the turning of the year, letting the light through so that the road was dappled with green shadows and patches of

177

brightness. The evening mist beginning to rise from the warm fields.

Small hills lined the road. Cows were grazing peacefully in a field of rushes, a donkey and cart left abandoned at the side of the road.

The driver turned.

'Looks like there might be an ambush ahead, sir. We should turn back.'

'We will not. Keep going. We'll give them as good as we get.'

Let me at them, he thought. The next time anyone tried to mock him for not being part of the fighting, he'd have his answer ready for them!

The ambushers had given up hope that Michael would pass that way. They were taking down the barricade when the convoy arrived, but the road was still partly blocked.

The convoy stopped.

Michael jumped from the car and pulled out his gun.

The blaze of the setting sun was against him as he started shooting. It made it hard to see what he was shooting at. He felt a surge of the old crazy feeling, that feeling of wild excitement. He'd knock that bully Denis Cadogan off him! There was no schoolmaster around to stop him now!

Shouts, curses, gunshots.

'Come on, lads!' shouted Michael. 'We'll get them on the run!'

There was another blast of fire. This time the fire was inside his head. Pain gripped him.

Michael fell.

It was very quick.

The light darkened and went out.

Michael had become part of the story.

Afterwards

*G*ive us our future, we have had enough of your past. Give us back our country to live in, to grow in, and to love.

Michael Collins

Ireland mourned when Michael Collins died. Even the hundreds of Republican prisoners held in Mountjoy Jail wept and prayed for him when they heard the news.

* * *

The Civil War continued, with enormous loss of life and savage atrocities committed on both sides. The Anti-Treaty army finally surrendered their arms in April 1923, but the Civil War left behind it a legacy of bitterness and division between those who had supported the Treaty and those who had fought against it. Northern Ireland continued to be part of the United Kingdom.

* * *

De Valera went back into government in 1930. He took the Oath of Allegiance, saying that it was by now an 'empty formula'. He then carefully began to unravel all the connections to the United Kingdom that were still in place. He died in 1972 after a long and distinguished career, probably the most influential politician of twentieth-century Ireland.

* * *

At the end of September, Nancy married Johnnie, and they moved to Dublin. Their first baby was called Michael. In later years, they lived near the De Valera family, and the families became good friends. They had an especially close friendship with Sinéad.

* * *

Maud and Gearóid got married in October. Kitty was there, dressed completely in black. Some years later, she married and had two sons, one of whom she called Michael.

* * *

Hannie said that even before she was given the news that Michael was dead and made the long and lonely journey across to Dublin for his funeral, she knew that something had happened. What she had felt was not foreboding or a feeling of fear, but a feeling of lightness, as if a burden had been lifted somewhere from Michael's shoulders. Later, she visited the spot where Michael had been shot. Cows grazed peacefully in the pasture beside the road, and a small brother and sister waved at her; they were on their way from the creamery, gathering late blackberries as they walked home. She thought of the words George Bernard Shaw had written to her, just after Michael's death:

I rejoice in his memory, and will not be so disloyal to it as to snivel over his death. So tear up your mourning and hang your brightest colours in his honour: and let us all praise God that he did not die in a snuffy bed of a trumpery cough, weakened by age, and sad-dened by the disappointments that would have attended his work had he lived.

Hannie took some comfort in his words. But they did not stop her missing her little brother.

Other Books from The O'Brien Press

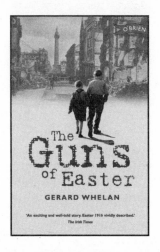

The Guns of Easter
Gerard Whelan

It is 1916 and Europe is at war. From the poverty of the Dublin slums twelve-year-old Jimmy Conway sees it all as glorious, and loves the British Army for which his father is fighting.

But when war comes to his own streets Jimmy's loyalties are divided. The rebels occupy the General Post Office and other parts of the city, and Jimmy's uncle is among them. Dublin's streets are destroyed, business comes to a halt.

In an attempt to find food for his family, Jimmy crosses the city, avoiding the shooting, weaving through the army patrols, hoping to make it home before curfew. But his quest is not easy and danger threatens at every corner.

Winner of the Bisto Book of the Year Eilís Dillon award — 1997
Winner of the Bisto Book of the Year Historical Novel — 1997

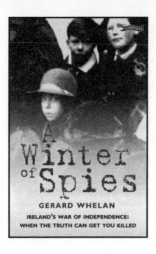

A Winter of Spies
Gerard Whelan

This sequel to the award-winning *The Guns of Easter* tells the exciting story of Sarah (Jimmy's young sister) and their family who are involved in the spying activities of Michael Collins during the War of Independence. Sarah, a young eleven-year-old, cannot figure out why her family is so neutral towards the war and why everybody is so secretive. A strong rebel herself, she wants to do her bit for Ireland. Then she finds out the terrible truth – and she too carries secrets which could cost her her life.

'excellent, a good story related straight as good stories deserve,
enjoyable at any age.'
Books Ireland

'thrilling ... adventures set against a completely realised period city,
and Sarah is a terrific heroine.'
RTÉ Guide

'The picture of a city and a period characterised by duplicity and deception is
excellently portrayed, as is Sarah herself, a remarkable feisty creation.'
The Irish Times

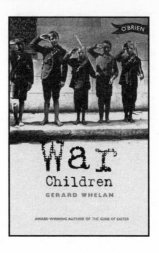

War Children
Gerard Whelan

Mattie Foley dreams of escaping the harshness of life in the Dublin slums, but her dreams and reality become dangerously entwined with the discovery of a gun.

When Statia Mulligan sets off to get feed for the hens, she longs for the peace and quiet of her favourite spot by the stream; she doesn't expect to become part of an ambush.

Larry Quinn goes after the cow that has strayed – how could he know that in his absence the Black and Tans would force his mother to reveal all she knows?

Six stories, one set in Dublin, the others in the countryside, about children who get caught up in the War of Independence and suffer dire consequences.

Winner of the Bisto Book of the Year Merit Award 2002–2003
Winner of the Reading Association of Ireland Award 2002–2003

'These stories ... are moving, thrilling and yet sometimes funny accounts of
events just a couple of generations removed from where we are now.'
Mary Arrigan – *Sunday Tribune*

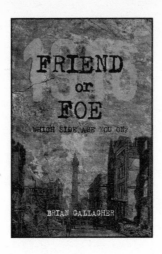

Friend or Foe
Brian Gallagher

It's time to choose: friendship, family or loyalty to the cause.

When Emer Davey saves her neighbour Jack Madigan from drowning, it seems that they will be friends forever. But eight months later, they find themselves on opposite sides in a life-or-death struggle, as Dublin is torn apart by the Easter Rising.

Emer's father is an officer in the Irish Volunteers who believes that armed rebellion is the only way to gain independence from Britain. His daughter has inherited his passion and is determined to help the rebels in any way she can.

Jack's dad is a sergeant in the Dublin Metropolitan Police. They share a deep respect for the law and are sure that Home Rule can be achieved through peaceful politics and helping with the war effort.

These two young friends find their loyalties challenged as the terrifying reality of war sets in – and the Rising hits closer to home than either could have imagined.

'beautiful writing, great character development, fascinating … a page-turner that is difficult to put down … a compelling and rewarding reading experience.'
The Irish Times

Pawns

Brian Gallagher

In a time of war, how much would you risk to help a friend?

Young Johnny Dunne works hard at Balbriggan's Mill Hotel, but still finds time to enjoy life with his friends, Alice and Stella. Though the three come from different backgrounds – Johnny had a harsh childhood in an orphanage, Alice is the daughter of the hotel owner, and Stella the daughter of the Commanding Officer at the nearby RAF Gormanston – they're inseparable, living at the hotel and playing together in the town band.

But with the War of Independence raging, the friends face difficult decisions. Stella is pro-British, Johnny is pro-independence, and Alice is somewhere in between.

Then Johnny's secret role, spying for the IRA, puts him in danger. And Stella and Alice have hard choices to make – choices that threaten their lives…

'an Irish historical novel for pre-teens that is both riveting and insightful. Perfect for individual or classroom reading'.

Sunday Independent

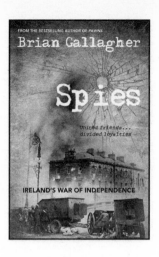

Spies
Brian Gallagher

In the sequel to *Pawns*, orphan Johnny Dunne has fled Balbriggan, where he spied for the rebels in Ireland's War of Independence. Now he has a new and even more dangerous mission. Rebel leader Michael Collins engages in a cut-throat secret war with British Intelligence: and Johnny, Ireland's youngest spy at only fourteen years of age, finds himself at the centre of the action. In a Dublin full of gunmen, soldiers, police inform- ers and the dreaded Black and Tans, Johnny has to watch his every move.

But it's hard to turn his back on the past, especially on his friendships with Alice Goodman, and with Stella Radcliffe, the daughter of a British officer, who risked her own life to save his.

As the War of Independence grows more lethal, the three friends must decide where their loyalties lie. Then a secret from Johnny's past changes everything...

'the strands of family and friendships are excellently interwoven with the fragile and fractious fault lines in pre-freedom Ireland.'
Irish Examiner

The Sound of Freedom
Ann Murtagh

It's spring 1919, and Ireland's War of Independence has broken out. In a cottage in County Westmeath, thirteen-year-old Colm Conneely longs to join the local Volunteers, the 'Rainbow Chasers' who are fighting for an Ireland free from English rule. But Colm has another ambition too – to make a new life in America, working as a fiddle player and involved in the republican movement there.

When spirited Belfast girl Alice McCluskey – who speaks Irish, shares his love of Irish music and is also committed to 'the cause' – arrives in town, Colm's dreams take a new turn. Where will his talent lead him? And how will a long-held family secret shape his future?

'action-packed … I just couldn't put it down.'
Ireland's Own Magazine

'well-crafted tale not only bringing Irish history to a new generation but entwining readers young and not-so young in a web of intrigue and family secrets.'
Evening Echo